More praise for ...and Other Disasters

Each of these imagined futures are alive with unnerving plausibility. Fans of thoughtful speculative fiction will relish this lyrical, emotional collection.

—Publishers Weekly

The stories of *...and Other Disasters* ask tough questions and envision answers that encompass not just a hypothetical future, but the present's trouble extrapolated to a nadir.

—Foreword Reviews

This collection by Malka Older may be mainly set in the future, but serves to show that people (whether they are human beings or alien or otherwise) will always stay the same. There is hope here, and loss, grief and joy. There is metaphor and poetry, song and data.

—Cathy Ulrich,
founding editor, Milk Candy Review

What a treasure this is! Malka Older shows enormous range in this collection of humane, thoughtful, and imaginative stories and poetry, showing why the term "speculative fiction" is such a great one. Older asks great questions and wraps them in fascinating characters.

—Sarah Pinsker,
author of *Sooner or Later Everything
Falls into The Sea* and *A Song For A New Day*

The best moments in *...and Other Disasters* achieve a rare combination in literature. They capture the fun (perfect memory recall, women in power!) in imagining what the future holds, and they capture the deep anxiety of imagining what the future holds (an Earth on the verge of rupture, a person's e-mails after death).

—Megan Giddings,
author of *Lakewood* and fiction editor of *The Offing*

Malka Older envisions futures of risk and possibility. Her political speculations are a reminder of what science fiction can do when it takes change seriously: each story in *...and Other Disasters* is a short, sharp reminder of the ephemerality of institutions we take for granted, and an embodiment of the truth that no authority is immortal or invulnerable.

—Ruthanna Emrys,
author of *Winter Tide*

Malka Older loves bizarre situations, but she never plays them for cheap thrills. She comes across like a psychoanalyst in a planetary refugee camp, and that's what makes her such a very modern science fiction writer.

—Bruce Sterling,
editor of *Mirrorshades
the Cyberpunk Anthology*

Exactly what we need right now, this is a book of beautiful fragments, tales of dying worlds and altered consciousnesses. It's not just stories, but a manual how to construct meaningful connections in an age of strife and disconnection, how to think, how to survive.

—Maxwell Neely-Cohen,
author of *Echo of the Boom*

...and Other Disasters

Malka Older

Mason Jar Press | *Baltimore, MD*

Published by
Mason Jar Press
Baltimore, MD 21218

Learn more about Mason Jar Press at masonjarpress.xyz.

Stories from the collection first appeard in the following publications: *Candidate Y* premiered, read aloud, on Mozilla's IRL podcast in an episode about elections and technology; *The End of the Incarnation* in Who Will Speak For America?, an anthology edited by Stephanie Feldman and Nathaniel Popkin; *The Black Box* as *The Black Box: These Memories are Made to Last Forever* in WIRED; *The Email Heiress* in Reservoir Lit; *The Rupture* in Capricious, Issue 3; and *Tear Tracks* on Tor.com.

...and Other Disasters

The Black Box

The Lifebrarian was installed just after Sumi's first birthday. Her grandparents insisted on paying for it. They insisted on the whole thing. Liliana was reluctant; she wanted her daughter to have the kind of life she still thought of as normal.

"It will probably affect the way her brain evolves," she argued to Hideyoshi. "Imagine if you never had to remember anything."

Hideyoshi didn't feel as strongly about it. A lot of people were having it done for their kids at that point. "She doesn't have to ever use the recall function if she doesn't want to."

"And she's so young to have surgery." Liliana's voice sounded as if she was pleading, and Sumi, too young to understand if not too young for surgery, looked up from her building blocks, eyes huge. It was one of the last moments in her life that would not be recorded, and as soon as Sumi's short-lived consciousness of it melted away, it was gone forever.

"It's minimally invasive," Hideyoshi reminded his wife. "There's barely any scar, and she's only under anesthesia for an hour." He didn't want to go up against Liliana's parents on this question. Besides, he could already see that Sumi's childhood was going by too fast for him.

Everyone talked about the operation like it was something you did for your kids, to arm them with the best bodyware for a highly competitive future. But Hideyoshi knew he wanted Sumi to have a Lifebrarian for purely selfish reasons. There was the immediate draw of being able to upload her feed at the end of the day and watch the world from her perspective, but overarching that was the reassuring thought that her quickly passing childhood would be stored somewhere, safe and sound and in high definition.

○ ○ ○

They disagreed again on when to tell her about it. Liliana wanted to wait as long as possible. "So she doesn't become self-conscious," she said.

Hideyoshi agreed that they should wait until she was old enough to understand, but also wanted to give her time to get used to the idea while she was still a child. "Can you imagine explaining this to her when she's a teenager and predisposed to be pissed off about anything we do?"

Like so many parenting decisions, this one was removed from their hands. When she was six years old, Sumi came home from school with the question "What's a Vidacorder?"

"Who mentioned that?" Liliana asked, looking up quickly from the vegetables she was chopping with Rosario, the cook.

"Beni says he has one," Sumi told her, sitting herself at the table. "And then Isa said she has one too, but Beni said it wasn't true."

"Ah." Liliana wiped her hand on her jeans and jotted a quick memo on her phone to remind herself which parents she could compare notes with.

"Do I have one?"

Offered the choice of prevarication, obfuscation, or truth, Liliana took refuge in one-upmanship. "You have a Lifebrarian, which is the same thing but better." She closed her eyes briefly, pausing her chopping; she could imagine the look Rosario was giving her without having to see it.

At least it stopped Sumi's questions for ten seconds while she thought about that. "How is it better?" she asked finally.

"Oh, higher resolution, better sound quality, easier uploading."

"Good," said Sumi.

○ ○ ○

"Mami," Sumi said, coming home from equestrian practice at age 12, "Esteban says that the Lifebrarian is like that little black box they have on airplanes, so that people know how I die. Is that true?"

"No!" Liliana gasped out. "Of course not, honey." She reached out for Sumi, but her daughter was already at the counter making herself a sandwich, as if what she had just asked didn't bother her at all.

"It's so people know how you live, sweetheart," Hideyoshi said, looking up from the news. "And I told you before, nobody has to see your recall feed unless you want them to."

Sumi considered this as she fished out a pickle, using her fingers as usual. "How will they know if I want them to, if I'm dead?"

Liliana pressed her fingers to her temple.

"I told you, you don't have to wait till you're dead," Hideyoshi said. "You can recall any time you want. It's just that your mother and I think it's better you wait till you're out of school before you start using that function."

"But what if I were dead?" Sumi went on. "What would happen to it?"

"You just have to make a note of who you want to be able to see it, if anyone," Liliana said, trying to show that it didn't bother her. "Legally, no one else can look."

The sandwich took priority. "I want you to be the one to look," Sumi said when it was gone. Her voice was aimed at a point between her parents, who exchanged a smile.

"We already have that right, as your parents," Liliana said, thinking this was comforting. "You don't have to worry about it at all until you're 21."

Sumi was silent then, but over the next nine years writing them out of her recorder-will was one of her most frequent threats.

○ ○ ○

"NO!" Sumi shouted, slamming her door. She couldn't help crying, and she imagined the Lifebrarian videofeed blurring. She threw herself onto her bed, squeezed her eyes shut, and thought of nothing as hard as she could. Black, black, black, like the screen after the movie ends in the split second before the ads start up again. Nothing, nothing, nothing.

She flipped over onto her back, her eyes still runny. It was a childish superstition, this belief that if she blanked out her mind hard enough and long enough it would erase what had just happened from the recorder if not from her life.

Sometimes she would even try to make a deal with the Lifebrarian, as if it were a person. As if it were God. "If you delete what just happened," she would mutter under her breath, "I'll talk all my thoughts out loud for a full day." Sumi knew that the recorder didn't care if she was good or bad. When she tried to bargain with it, more of herself was all she could think to offer.

It was all a silly way of thinking, a leftover from when she was small and believed the Lifebrarian was an actual person, sitting inside her skull, wielding an old-fashioned video camera.

At 16 she could be smarter than that. What she should really do was start thinking as blandly as possible before bad things happened, as soon as she started feeling cranky or evil, and make her life totally boring so that whoever watched it would fast-forward and maybe miss the bad stuff.

If only she could know when bad things were about to happen.

○ ○ ○

Sumi was hoping for a loophole. Surely the Lifebrarian didn't record while she was using recall, right? Four days earlier she had used the recall function to relive her first truly complete sexual experience, which had taken place two days before that, and since then she had replayed it so many times that anyone watching the repeats would know she was a nympho. Why would the recorder waste memory rerecording what it already had?

Of course there was memory to spare in that sliver-thin chip next to her skull. Enough for four extended lifetimes, her dad had told her once. That idea gave her the creeps, the thought of it recording blankness for years and decades and centuries, nothing after nothing, more nothing than any human being could ever watch in its entirety. But that wouldn't happen; there was some sort of trigger to cut recording when her heart stopped pumping. She didn't want to think about that either.

○ ○ ○

Sumi is 44 and 25,000 feet above Johannesburg when she decides to get the black box upgrade for her Lifebrarian. There's not even any turbulence, but landings always make her nervous, and she starts to think about what will happen if they crash.

The black box protective casing will make accessing the recall function a little more complicated, but Sumi doesn't use recall much anyway. She doesn't have time to be mooning over memories. Maybe when the kids are grown and she's retired she'll want to look back more, but then she can have it adjusted again, and the technology will probably have improved too. Besides, her wife has her own recorder, and both kids have the latest versions: smaller, faster, and complete with real-time brain scans. If she ever wants to remember a moment, it's almost certain to have other witnesses who can do the recall themselves.

Unless she dies while alone on a business trip, like right now. For anyone to know what happens in that case, she needs her recorder to be protected from fire, massive trauma, or water immersion for up to six months, as they say in the vidpitch.

They also make it sound like it's something you do for your family, because after all, you won't be around to watch the replay. But Sumi wonders about that. Is it really that different for your wife or children if the last contact they have with you is when you say "I love you" before hanging up the phone or if they can see the end of your life right up to the blunt trauma of your last moment? Either way there's an end, and grief.

No, she thinks, the black box is for her, so that she will know in that second of consciousness before she goes that someone will be able to see exactly what happened to her.

If she dies violently. If not, well, it won't make any difference. The black box upgrade is just a precaution, like life insurance. Hopefully she won't need it, but it's good to have in case she does.

The upgrade is a simple operation, minimally invasive. They don't even need anesthesia for it; Sumi just sits in a comfortable chair watching vids while they do it. Kind of like being on a plane, she thinks at one point, but they've asked her to try to relax and use her brain as little as possible, so she concentrates on the vids.

It's not that she doesn't intend to tell her wife, Kara, but one day after another it just doesn't happen. The operation was so easy that Sumi almost forgot about it herself once it was over. There is no scar for anyone to ask about, and every time she opens her mouth to bring it up the subject just seems out of place. She can imagine Kara's face as she makes the morbid connection between the upgrade and what it's meant for. She sees Kara trying to hide her worry while the kids ask loud, insensitive questions about what it is, about why they don't have one, sees her pressing her palm to her forehead. There's just no need.

It almost comes up a couple of times when there are questions about the past: at Lili's school film, at a fundraiser after a hurricane hits in the north, at a work seminar. But each time Sumi pretends to fumble with something else or be distracted for a moment, and each time someone else does recall and finds the answer first. It's really not that hard to do recall with the black box, just a little awkward in a way that people might notice. The very few times when she personally wants to remember a time, a place, she also resists. This is what it was like to live before, she tells herself; this is how my grandparents lived their whole lives.

She's glad she got the upgrade, even if she never really has to use it. Even if her loved ones never really have to use it. If she dies quietly in her bed, they'll never even have to know she had it done. And if she dies violently, well, they'll know exactly how.

○ ○ ○

As it turns out, Sumi does die violently, some 12 years later. However, an estimated 14,000 other people die in the same earthquake. There are tent cities, there are aftershocks, there are rapidly dug mass graves. There is no time to delve into anyone's last moments. Not even rich people's.

For the tenth anniversary memorial, a committee of family and survivors does gather (meaning exhume, for the most part) what recorders can be salvaged. Sumi's is displayed, tastefully, along with the others, but it is inert: a sliver of dead circuitry centered in a glass case. Some of the newer models survived the long wait and are played on endless loops in the experience rooms, but the older hardware of Sumi's Lifebrarian has long since been corrupted.

The End of the Incarnation I

California was the first. It was dicey for a few months, with threats of war and loud talk of treason, but when some financial and trade benefits were made clear to the central executive, all hints of aggression were quickly walked back, as if they had never been.

The other risk to the hypothetical new country was internal. Towns, counties, and regions disagreed, wanting to remain or wanting to separate even further. For a while it looked like San Francisco would become its own nation, and for a few weeks the betting markets had separate Northern and Southern Californias as a favorite scenario, reaching as high as 10–1. The problem of where to draw the line between Northern and Southern scuttled that option, and the final vote led to a complete, single-state secession.

The Rupture

There was a rupture a few cycles before Exelle went to Earth for the first time. It was just a small one, far from populated areas and, most importantly (as Exelle explained to her mother and friends), predicted.

"The only casualties were because people actually went to watch," she told them. "Everyone who wanted to avoid it did, but some idiots wanted to see the lava flows up close, and even in that group only a few were caught in it."

"You won't do that, will you?" her mother asked.

"Of course not!" Exelle said. She wasn't going to Earth to chase after thrills or to prove anything.

"So why are you going?" her soul-friend Saiwai asked, when Exelle repeated the conversation with her. "I mean, no matter what you say, it's dangerous."

"It's where we come from." Exelle answered as emphatically as she could. Her own conviction was fading in proportion to the drastic news coverage of the rupture.

"Yeah, and there's a reason we left," Saiwai said. "The whole planet is going to fall apart."

"Not for hundreds of cycles!" The problem was, of course, that nobody knew exactly when; it could be in hundreds of cycles, it could be next cycle. But most experts said hundreds, and Exelle thought the fact that they had accurately (or almost accurately) predicted the place and time of the latest rupture was a good sign.

And so she went. She was signed up and her ticket was paid and everyone knew she was going, so however many urgent last-breath fears she had, however strong that sense of certainty that she was committing time-delayed suicide, she had to go. Or so she told herself, and so she went.

One of the commitments that kept her going was the acceptance to Xinsibirsk Dashu, the best university (left) on Earth. She landed there on a warm late winter morning, woozy from the long space journey and the worry, barely able to note the strange smells that her ancestors' noses had evolved in tandem with, the strange angle of the sunlight. The strange everything, really. She crawled into the capsule assigned to her in the extraterrestrials' dorm and slept until she woke up.

The classes and the routine helped her manage the sense of strangeness for a while. There were relatively few extraterrestrials at that point, with the (overblown, everyone assured her) concerns about the ruptures and eventual orbital instability, but there had been a time when many came to experience a few cycles on Earth, and the facilities still existed to make them feel at home. She could live almost like she was still on Sebrang, if she wanted to. But Exelle discovered a thirst for difference. She turned off her translator sometimes, in class; at first for a vertiginous few moments of incomprehension, and then (after she discovered the subtitles function) for longer periods, until she started to pick out familiar words through the antiquated rhythms.

She started trying out Earthling words on her Earthling classmates. It was hard to tell which were friends, and which were just people willing to talk to her about her research. Exelle was warned before she left about how "friendly" Earthlings could be, how their culture was very direct and hospitable and expressive, and she shouldn't misinterpret it. The Sebrang Encyclopedia of Interplanetary Anthropology was the most explicit about it, in language that Exelle found positively xenophobic: "Many visitors" (no citation!) "have reported that after being received with overwhelming smiles and invitations, they were disappointed to be betrayed in large or small ways by their Earthling hosts, to the point of wondering whether they were welcome there at all."

Exelle's favorite anthropology professor back on Sebrang had made it clear that they could pretty much assume they weren't welcome, wherever they went. "Who really likes being studied?" she would ask the class rhetorically. "Okay, there is some novelty, maybe even some glamour, in having someone so interested in you. But with time you will start to wonder why. What is it about you that is so freakish or foreign that it deserves methodological examination?"

Exelle was not, then, completely naïve when she arrived on Earth. But even with these layers of warning, she found it difficult to figure out how to act around Earthlings. They were very friendly, very warm. People she had barely nodded to in class would call out from the other end of the atmoshield, waving their pale Earthling arms at her. In study circles there was an unexpected amount of touching—elbows joshing elbows, taps on knees or shoulders.

It was also hard to calibrate because at the same time, Exelle's feelings about herself had changed.

At home, she was just on the gangly edge of normal size, almost too tall, sometimes awkward. Here, she was tiny, petite, delicate. She was also darker than most Earthlings. They smiled at her more than people smiled at her at home, and she had to keep reminding herself that they smiled at everyone more than people did at home. All this combined to make her feel far more attractive than usual. When people stared at her as she walked around campus, she wasn't sure whether it was because she was an extraterrestrial or whether, maybe, it was because they wanted to touch her.

She did try to keep on professional ground with her research assistant, Starfish. Exelle spent the first cycle or two wondering which of his personal characteristics had led to that nickname, but then she learned that it had been, at various times in Earth history, trendy for parents to name their newborns after species that had recently gone extinct. Thus (among the Earthlings in her classes or that Starfish introduced her to) Lepidopter; Pacifica; Anteater. Some of these names were then passed down from generation to generation, resulting in Tigers and Honeybees that were centuries away from having cohabited the planet with their namesakes.

The campus canteens, especially the Mars Bar (amazing how these offensive jokes persisted), had ingredients shipped in from other planets, meaning that Exelle could consume at least fairly decent approximations of what she was used to. But long before Starfish hesitantly suggested it, Exelle knew from her background reading that food was very important in Earthling culture, and that she needed to take potential interviewees out to eat.

At first she found their limited cuisine mildly distasteful, especially the cheap food available near the university: greasy, heavy dogmeat deep-fried in egg yolk, or barley pancakes dripped with chemical sugar. But people would always ask her how she liked it, and Exelle was not talented at polite lies, as these were not particularly valued on Sebrang. Eventually Starfish and Ybor, another occasional translator, found a couple of restaurants she could actually look forward to. There was a vegetarian place not far from her dorm that had simple but tasty dishes, and a bar called Pijo a few blocks further away, nearer to the town proper, that did creative and artificial flavoring-free renditions of various traditional dishes. It was there, too, that Exelle learned about beer.

Alcohol had the status of an illegal drug on Sebrang, although moderate use was tolerated in certain subsets of the human community, and Exelle had never had more than a surreptitious sip or two. She didn't understand the point of it, and certainly not why it might be worth time in penitentiary, especially since it was well known that alcohol could also make people violent and unhappy. The bar made her very nervous the first time she went in; not only did everyone have alcoholic drinks in front of them, but most of them were armed, something which never, she told Starfish in undertones, happened on Sebrang.

"It's fine, don't worry so much," he told her, but the fear of being killed in an indiscriminate bar brawl layered over the fear, always with her since she had arrived, of dying in an unexpected rupture or the apocalypse. The interview went badly, as Exelle kept losing focus to dart her eyes around the room looking for early warning signs, and she went home early, slept poorly, and missed her first two classes the next morning.

Starfish was hesitant to take her to Pijo again, but when another interview subject (a woman from whose family at least one person had emigrated in each of the past twenty generations) suggested it as a meeting point, Exelle insisted that they go.

She didn't drink, and still felt on guard the whole time, but she was able to see that the Earthlings were relaxed and enjoying themselves and that no one was worried about the weapons. After that, they did a number of interviews there, and eventually, goaded by the amused comments from interviewees, Exelle even learned to manage half a glass of beer. Starfish assured her it had relatively little alcohol, only 30%.

It was also at Pijo that she first used a spoon; on Sebrang, due to the physiology of the native inhabitants, food was usually consumed more directly. She had read about spoons before, of course, but it was not until she saw two of them slotted together that she suddenly understood the derivation of the Earthling idiom for "lying curled together." It was a usage that she had learned recently.

During the second half of her time on Earth, Exelle had no classes, and was expected to spend all her time on her research. Before her time in the classroom completely ended though, she started dating an Earthling she had been exchanging glances with all semester. At first she was cautious with him, aware that even with the help of the automatic translators and body language annotators there could be misunderstandings, aware that Earthlings ("living closer to death" as the Encyclopedia of Anthropology noted with unhelpful, unsubstantiated interpretation) had a culture more accepting of easy sexual relations. But Linsed was respectful and careful, and Exelle enjoyed her time with him. Once, he told her that she was not his first extraterrestrial relationship, which immediately made her wonder if he had an extraterrestrial fetish, or if he was looking for an emigration ticket. In any case, she told herself, she didn't think it was a relationship destined for the long-term.

Occasionally she would wonder, completely out of context, what exactly were the large and small ways in which previous visitors had been betrayed by Earthlings. If the encyclopedia was going to be so folkloric, it ought to include the stories and examples, she thought.

She was careful not to talk about or display her relationship in front of Starfish, since she suspected him, with his courteousness and thoughtfulness, of harboring a crush on her. They would be working ever more closely together during the research phase of her study, and she didn't want to confuse things, or upset him. Then, as her Earthling language comprehension got better, she overheard him one day talking with an interview subject about his family. She had never thought of him as married.

When a new rupture was forecast, it was the talk of the campus. Everyone was making plans to go. "It's like a carnival," Linsed told her. "Come on, it'll be great!" The rupture was predicted to occur in the middle of the ocean, not far from where the ancient city of Jakarta lay under the surface, and Linsed was eager to get some diving in while they were there.

"Diving? At the site of a predicted rupture? You must be crazy," Exelle told him, and stormed off.

But everyone was talking about it, everyone was going. When Exelle heard that Starfish was not only going, but would be taking his two small children with him, she relented and told Linsed they could go. Because she was still a little nervous, she told him they were going to stay in one of the expensive pop-up hotels rather than camping in the university atmosphere shield that was being set up. He seemed almost disappointed by this, even when she told him she'd pay the full bill, and when they got there she could understand why: the carnival was definitely in the landing strip-sized, bubble-shaped shields that were being moored all around the predicted location, and not in their hotel, where most of the guests were middle-aged to elderly. But the rupture hadn't happened yet, and Exelle was just as happy to sleep in the quiet, heavily reinforced hotel and spend the jumpy days out in the university atmoshield.

As the days went by everyone got a bit more nervous. During the burning afternoons, as they listened to bands or courted various kinds of highs on the fake grass of the atmoshield, the students whined that if the rupture didn't happen soon they'd have to go back to class and miss it. Exelle suspected they were anxious for it to occur soon because the last rupture predictions were off by thirteen miles and two days, and the further this one got from its forecast date, the more they worried about distance from the predicted location. The atmoshields were built to take the waves, but were not so well constructed as to be immune to lava explosions. (If she thought about it, Exelle had to admit that the hotel probably wouldn't survive a direct hit either, but it would do better with a close miss).

From the due date on, Linsed insisted on sleeping at the atmoshield with his classmates.

"I don't want to miss it if it happens at night," he said. "Especially if it happens at night." Everyone was hoping for a nighttime event; the first lava flows were apparently the most spectacular, and of course they were more visible in the darkness. But Exelle still preferred the hotel. Every tremor, whether caused by seismic activity or by an ocean swell, sent adrenaline clutching through her gut.

It happened during the day, although at least late enough that the swollen sun was no longer directly overhead. There was a rumble, a huge rumble, so much bigger than the previous tremors that Exelle thought it must be qualitatively different, she thought: They were wrong, it isn't a rupture, it is *the* rupture, the planet is about to fly into pieces and be sucked into the sun. I'm going to die here. Everyone around her stood up, there was an excited crescendo of murmurs, and Exelle tried to read in their eyes whether it was all anticipation or whether some of them, too, feared for their lives. But then, off to their east against a sky that was already darkening, after an extra, portentious shudder, the sky was split by red fire. It spun up into the air, twisting and spiring, a pyrotechnic wall. Exelle watched it, her breath still coming short and quick with fear. When the barge shook again she grabbed Linsed's arm, startled, and he grabbed back and pulled her to him and kissed her, and she felt the dissociation of wondering how anyone could think a rupture signaling the end of a planet was romantic while at the same time picturing their silhouette against that scintillating background. This is something living people shouldn't see, she thought, the planet is dying, without support systems everyone would be dead by now, people aren't supposed to survive this. But for the moment, at least, they had.

The eruptions went on for days, and it was only then that the party really started to make sense to Exelle. The biggest musicians only came in once the rupture began, the most famous artists, the greatest circus acts. There was one band that only played songs about the end of the world; there were fire-eaters who lit their torches with lava brought in fresh from the rupture; there were fortune-tellers (none of the predictions she heard, Exelle noted, included a long life) and acrobats. Everything became more crowded and expensive, now that it was relatively safe, and she felt absurdly glad that she experienced the pre-rupture days, even if she didn't fully enjoy them. She also felt okay with going back to Xinsibirsk and getting back to work, and she was happy she could finally stop lying to her mother about where she was. She waited a couple of weeks to break up with Linsed, not wanting him to think it was because of the rupture, because that seemed silly. Anyway, there were only a few cycles before she went home.

The night before she left, Starfish and Ybor took her to a Japanese restaurant. Japan had, of course, been submerged for centuries. The owner of the restaurant, a man of Japanese descent, had been born in Inner San Francisco, leaving as an infant only a few months before it, too, was destroyed. He came to their table before the meal, while they were nibbling on yuzu-walnut bread rolls, to tell them about how he had revived old family recipes through a combination of genetic engineering and chemical manipulation to replace ingredients that no longer existed, on Earth or anywhere else. Exelle wished she could take a roll back to Sebrang for Saiwai to taste. She wished she could take the whole meal. Or bring Saiwai here, just to taste it once, just to understand what her ancestors had eaten.

"It's too bad you're leaving now," Ybor said. A new prediction had come out of a rupture that was scheduled to happen in the middle of what had once been North America, and everyone was excited because there hadn't been a rupture on land in almost a century. "Are you sure you can't stay a little longer?"

"I really can't," Exelle lied. A land rupture! That would probably be what finally destroyed the planet. Then she asked them what she had asked all of her informants. "Why don't you leave?"

They just looked at her, not understanding the sudden change of subject.

"I mean, why don't you emigrate? You could, you know." She wished she could take them back with her. She wished fervently, more than anything (in honor of the farewell, she had drunk more than usual) that she could save them.

Ybor shrugged. "My home is here."

"You could make your home somewhere else," Exelle said, starting to feel desperate. "You have no future here. This planet is dying."

Starfish was smiling, twisting his cup in his long fingers. "Not yet. Probably not while I'm alive, maybe not even in my children's lifetimes. And if we go somewhere else, we won't have the freedoms we have here."

Incomprehensible. "What do you mean? What freedoms?"

"To live the way we want to."

"You can live the way you want on Sebrang, on another planet!"

Ybor tilted his head at her. "Come on. Aren't you a little like..." he searched for the phrase. "Second-class citizens?"

Exelle was stunned. She had never in her life thought of herself that way. "No, it's not like that at all, it's, it's just..."

Starfish leaned forward. "You are on someone else's planet, right? You have to live in what's left, what they don't want."

"Not exactly, I mean, there are the Accords, and we live...we live just fine..." Was this how they had seen her the whole time?

"Don't most people work as servants for the Brangers?" Ybor asked.

"Just—some. And they're not exactly servants, they—" Exelle struggled for words. Did they pity her? Did they actually feel sorry for emigrants? "There's nothing wrong with—the way we live, in fact it's—it's great, it's—" She stopped again, catching herself before she said 'better.' It would be rude, and she didn't think they would believe her anyway.

"There's nothing wrong with it," Starfish said. "But that's not how I want to live."

Briefly, Exelle no longer wanted to take them back with her. As they stumbled back towards the university, Ybor leaned in to her, a little too close and smelling of rediscovered plum wine, to whisper that he had saved his genetic material in the interplanetary gene bank, just in case. Exelle could only shake her head. On Sebrang it had been centuries since cloning was considered anything but futile, and extremely gauche.

By the next morning, when she said goodbye in front of the spaceport, she was already thinking herself silly. The land rupture would probably be fine, meaning not the end of the world, and it would be amazing to see. And certainly there was something different here on Earth, she wouldn't call it freedom exactly, but there was something, maybe something about belonging. Or maybe, as the encyclopedia said, living closer to death. She still thought Starfish and Ybor were crazy, but she hugged them both and cried a little once she had already turned away. And she started thinking about coming back. Maybe. Someday. She was starting to have an idea for another research project, one about how Earthlings perceived extraterrestrials. She was pretty sure she could get funding to come back for that. If, of course, Earth survived the land rupture. If Earth survived. For the moment Exelle was just happy that she had.

It wasn't until many dozens of cycles and many terrified, fascinating visits later that Exelle realized that the real danger of her first visit wasn't immediate death by rupture. No, the risk that first time had been the sly creep of Earth-love into her blood, this twinned urge to leave and pining to return, this addiction that kept her coming back again and again and that might yet prove fatal.

Compost

This loam is rich with lance-split bone, and silt,
With rotting tomes, soft mulch, and chrome, with rust
And blood, and silicone, decayed pulp crushed
By stone, and drowning cats, and delayed guilt.

The soil is flushed; this is where people killed,
In all this rebuilt land packed and encrust
With dirt, soft-crammed detritus and dust.
Search if you will these guts, sift soil and filter:

There is no earth that's never been a corpse.
It breathes with cemeteries themselves buried,
Remnants of cells that lived and died, nourished,
Inhabited, and died again, carrion
We feasted on and fed, the sudden flourish
Of roses, turnips, snuffling beasts, and stories.

The End of the Incarnation II

Texas was next, which surprised some non-Texans because that state had no particular problem with the way the federal level was being run, but once the prospect of nationhood was out there, a plurality of Texans couldn't turn it down. Texas voted for independence, then immediately established close political and financial ties to its old country, and went on, for the moment, much as it was. Montana did the same.

The states of the eastern seaboard dithered longer, believing size still mattered. Four of New York City's boroughs were fueled with a burst of righteous anger after California's successful separation, but that was tempered by the rest of the state, until finally the city decided to slice itself away. This proved somewhat messier than the other secessions, as deals had to be worked out around a number of cross-border services (New Jersey Transit almost went defunct), but it inspired (or shamed) Massachusetts into seceding too.

The Divided

The walls rose anyway.

They couldn't build them. They'll never do it, there's no humanly possible way they can do it in any reasonable amount of time with any reasonable amount of money, that's what my tía Lola had been saying since the idea appeared, and she wasn't wrong. But they rose anyway, crawling their way to the sky like thornbushes, like sudden ramparts, like instant slices of mesa.

My abuela was caught in one on her way to work. That's how we knew they rose so quickly, because it caught her in mid-stride. On Sundays we went to visit her. My father rubbed baby oil into the heel of her left foot, raised slightly out of the back of her work pumps. "Qué lástima, that you were caught in those uncomfortable shoes." He talked to her all the time, although since we couldn't see her ears, I was pretty certain she couldn't hear him. He rubbed Nivea into the creases of her right elbow, pushed back with the weight of the black leather purse we knew was tucked under her arm, only a corner of it visible below her elbow. Sometimes my mother would come with a bucket of water and shampoo and undo the last twist of bun that protruded from the wall. She would wash the three inches of grey hair, the very ends of my abuela's long hair that normally would sway at her waist and now only fluttered from the wall like a sad flag. Then she would pat them dry with a marigold-yellow towel and wrap the bun up again.

"So unfortunate that she was caught facing that way," my father would sigh, because my abuela barely spoke English, and we imagined that they didn't allow Spanish over there anymore.

We imagined because we didn't know. No stories came out. We didn't know if my abuela was worse off, or my prima Letty, who was trapped somewhere on the inside. She wasn't in the wall: my tío César went all the way around it looking for her, meter by meter. He thought he would be able to sneak in somewhere, but the walls went all the way around. The river was all fucked up, he told us when he came back, and the ocean crashed against walls now: no more beaches, no more cliffs. He held out some hope that he would be able to cross in from Canada, but the walls had risen there too, trapping people and cars, even a few border agents. He didn't find Letty in the wall, so she had to be on the inside. We waited. Surely they would deport people, but no one appeared. Maybe they couldn't figure out how to get them through the wall.

No stories came out, and yet we had stories. Some people said they had done it on purpose, found some new chemical-industrial witchcraft. Others said it was a judgment on them, even when it felt more like a judgment on us. Analysts predicted war and anarchy, said that inside the crops would be failing and people would be starving and squabbling. That was hard to grasp though, all that money and power rotting away so quickly. It was easier to imagine that inside they were engineering monsters or killer robots, triaging their victims expertly by melanin content or neuro-linguistic pathways. We imagined them coming for us, clawing their way through the wall or marching along a path that opened for them at the touch of a button, because surely they had a way to get through. We imagined them coming for us in tanks and F-16s, followed by our lost relatives and friends transformed into a zombie army. We imagined this happening, and then we made movies about it: blob monsters fermented from a stew of nitrates and untreated sewage; super-soldiers without hearts or cavities, all steely eyes and square jaws.

Instead what came was what they call blight. People started moving away, not because of fear but because there were few jobs and no buyers from the north and nothing coming down from the north to buy, and then once people started moving there were fewer jobs. My father had to close his barbershop, but he was hired at the hotel where my mother worked, because the one industry that remained was tourism. I sold flowers at a little stand near the wall, for people to leave by the edges of their loved ones or in memory of those who were unreachable.

The first time someone asked me about the best flowers for the wall itself I didn't understand the question. I shook my head and wrote that señora off as one more person detached from reality, but people kept asking. I went to look and found shrines that were not dedicated to the lost but to the walls themselves. People were praying that the walls would keep us safe from chemical-stained water and fracking earthquakes and particle-ridden air. I decided the flower for this was a cactus, and over the next years we sold so many I had to start a cactus garden. But when people told me they wanted to pray the walls would keep us safe from other contaminants, from xenophobia and hate and fear, then I told them the appropriate flower was roses. Anyone foolish enough to believe walls can keep you safe from those things deserved to pay for our most expensive bloom.

We stayed for six years, until my abuela died. I knew as soon as I saw her that Sunday, it was an instant impression like a flashbulb, but I didn't want to look at my father to see if I was right. When we got closer we could see those knobs of skin my father used to care for so cariñosamente had changed color, gone pale and purpley, and when we touched her—my father clinging to her fragment of heel with two fingers and a thumb while I pressed one fingertip to her elbow—she was cold. My father curled down and put his head on the ground and cried, cried for so long I started to feel sick, as if the world were spinning too fast and I didn't know what to do.

There are worse stories than ours, but I don't want to tell them. Newlyweds and newborns and dying relatives of all varieties. People who did everything they could and some things that nobody could do, and none of it helped. There are many worse stories, but I don't want to tell them. I wish I'd never heard them, that they had never happened.

We buried my abuela in the way that had become custom, patting soil over her sad hard heel and her elbow, patting it into a mound sloping out from the wall that covered a more or less human shape, and leaving a little memorial stone for her at the bottom. For a while my father still went every Sunday to leave flowers and to cry.

Then we moved south. Tío César and Tía Lola stayed in case anyone ever came through, anyone they could ask about what happened on the other side. They were hoping to have a guess about the rest of their daughter's life, even if she never got out herself. Mainly they were hoping to be reassured that it wasn't as anguished as what they imagined.

But we moved south. I didn't think it would ever happen, because my father was so sad. The only reason he managed it finally was for me. "You should forget," he whispered to me, the night after we crossed the desert and reached the first city that looked like a real city. We were staying in a tiny hotel, we could hear snores from the rooms next to us, the rushing of water when someone flushed a toilet on the floor above, and, from the bar down the street, cumbia and sometimes bachata. "You should forget and live your life." I nodded when he said that, because even though they always taught us to study history and remember injustice and never forget, I couldn't find any lesson here that would help me be anything but sad.

Some people are afraid now, with all that's going on, that the walls will grow again, to the south of us this time. There are those who are in favor, saying it is such a tiny border we need to close, a totally different situation, but others say that if they rise they won't just keep out the guatemaltecos and catrachos but will continue all along the coasts until they meet the impenetrable walls in the north. Then we'll be the ones shut in and quarantined from the world. Others scoff and say we are still a long way from that happening, it's only talk and not nearly as bad as it was back there, back then. Some still pray to the walls in the north, rogando that algún día they will fall away and we will find a healed land within. Maybe a healed people too, although as time passes that idea is fading.

Me, I keep my eyes on the colors in front of me: mangos and tejidos and pink pickled onions, limones and azulejos and the potholes in the road. I listen for music, any kind of twang or resonance, any beat, and especially the voices that climb in sobbing crescendos. I trail my fingertips along the stone and concrete of buildings, knowing I could be caught at any breath, trapped for the rest of my life between one imagined country and another.

Expatriat

The leaves fall early this year.
Not enough wind to carry the ashes this far.
We might detect an unexplained creaking. The streams
of deconstructed letters under uncaring seas
leave new gaps, a space for disaster between each beat.
A tremor in the electricity, a miscarried connection
and the news may be traceless vanished or wrong.
Here the markets haven't trembled prices aren't affected.
We slept through all the comets, and the eclipses
obscured some point on the opposite side of the earth.
I raise my head to the full moon,
but find instead the sun teary and unrayed in the
impenetrable sky
These days we are far from home
with no clearer omens of disaster
than the stiff phantom photos on silent screens
and the sudden agglomeration of chirping birds
waiting in the winter sky.

The End of the Incarnation III

After that, the rest of the northeast coast removed itself in irregular succession. The longest and bloodiest fight for independence was in the District of Columbia, where daily riots and the chant of "taxation without representation" hampered government business for months. The problem in DC was not only its prestige and symbolic value. When other states had separated, they had taken their representatives with them, tipping what was left of the United States toward a stronger consensus; DC had no representatives, no official opposition voices that would disappear with its separation. Finally, the ruling party convinced itself that it was an acceptable territorial loss. The government of the United States decamped for Kansas City and watched its territory shrink as its mandate grew.

Tear Tracks

Nobody expected them to look human. If anyone still harbored that kind of anthropocentric bias, they kept it bottled up with their other irrational fantasies (or nightmares) of successful contact. The biophysicists had theorized alternative forms that could support higher intelligence: spiraling cephalopods, liquid consciousness, evenly-distributed sentience. The Mission Director, who was known for being broad-minded, even invited some science fiction writers to work with the scientists in imagining what intelligent alien life might look like. The collaboration didn't generate many usable ideas for the Mission (although it did lead to half a dozen best sellers and a couple of ugly lawsuits). And after all that thought and effort and retraining of assumptions, the first intelligent extraterrestrial life-forms they found were humanoid.

Not completely human, not like actors in silver face paint, but bilaterally symmetrical, bipedal, with most of the sensory organs concentrated in a central upper appendage that was difficult not to call the head.

"We need a new word, a whole new vocabulary," Tsongwa said, as he and Flur reviewed hours and hours of long-distance surveillance video. "A term to remind us that they're not human, but still give them equal importance and intelligence."

Because not only were they humanoid (the word did not satisfy Tsongwa, but it caught on and stuck), they were clearly intelligent, with societies and civilizations. They lived not in the caves or intelligent-organic complexes or mind-alterable environments hypothesized by the scientists, but in identifiable buildings, in cities. (The Mission Director promptly brought in architects, urbanists, psychologists, forensic archeologists, urban psychologists, forensic architects). They were "advanced" (Tsongwa insisted on putting the word in quotes) enough that first contact with them could be via radio, and then video. Many of the linguistic problems, not to mention the initial shock of alien existence, could be worked out long before Flur and Tsongwa got anywhere near the planet.

The Mission Director insisted on the importance of a protocol for contact, flexible enough to use in as many different contexts as they could imagine (an optimist, he was still hoping to discover intelligent spiraling cephalopods), yet structured enough to allow for some degree of standardization. Two ambassadors, one male, one female (the Mission Director did not point out that they were also of different "races," another word Tsongwa used only in quotes). They would go armed, but imperceptibly so. They would go with scientific objectives—as much observation and recording as possible—but also with diplomatic goals that were more important: they were to bring back, if not a treaty, at least an agreement. "A framework," the Mission Director explained, "for future relations." He made a template for them, but encouraged them to modify it as necessary. The next day he came back with a few more templates, to give them a sense of the range of options.

Flur, the brilliant young star of what they call the Very Foreign Service, smiles and nods, but he's overselling it. She's pretty sure she can figure out the acceptable options, maybe even some the Mission Director hasn't come up with, just as she's pretty sure she can charm these aliens by respecting and listening to them, by empathizing, by improvising. Maybe more than Tsongwa. She likes Tsongwa, but he's so serious, and places too much importance on semantics. She knows he's supposed to be the experienced balance to her youth and genius, but nobody's experienced anything like this before. And he's not actually that much older; it's just the deep lines on his face and the slow pace of his consideration that make him seem so.

Flur is aware of another probable advantage: as far as they have been able to tell, most of the alien leadership is female. Or the equivalent of female, what looks like female to the humans, which means human females will look like leaders to the aliens. Even Flur's skin color is closer to the rosy purple of alien flesh. Though no one has mentioned either of these cultural elements, Flur prepares herself for the possibility that she will need to act as the head of the expedition, even if she remains technically subordinate to Tsongwa.

Her confidence, or overconfidence, does not pass unnoticed. But it doesn't worry the Mission Director or Tsongwa much. Flur is never disrespectful, and she works hard, studying the video and audio recordings, diagramming and re-diagramming what they understand about political structures, writing short treatises about cultural practices.

The time and place of the landing are set, and there is a flashy ceremony for the departure from the base station, full of flags and symbols and fine music, scripted and simulcast. Flur has an odd longing to wave to her mother, but manages to quell it. Fortunately, the Mission Director has managed to fend off requests to simulcast the mission itself (largely by reminding politicians and media executives about the unlikely but real possibility of a grisly end to the adventure). The closing air lock leaves Flur and Tsongwa alone, except for the eighty-two mission staff looped into their communications and recording network. They beam down, a slang phrase for what is in practice a long, bumpy, and dangerous trip into the planet's atmosphere on a shuttle known as the Beamer. This is Tsongwa's expertise, and Flur is appropriately grateful for it as she copilots. He ably navigates them to the designated landing site, an extensive field outside of the alien city.

Flur takes a deep breath once they are settled. Through the small window she can make out tall, curving shapes: the aliens, the natives of this planet, have gathered as planned. From the screen on the dash the Mission Director looks back at her, almost bathetic in the way emotion and overwhelming awareness of the significance of this moment play openly on his face. Flur checks her comms and stands up. For a moment she and Tsongwa are face-to-face in the narrow aisle between the seats, and though his chin is level with her forehead Flur feels for the first time that they are looking straight at each other. This moment, though it is being recorded and transmitted in a dozen different sensory and technological combinations, is still theirs alone. There is a mutual nod—Flur doesn't know which of them initiates it—and then Tsongwa leads the way to the hatch.

Stepping out of the Beamer, Flur finds that the aliens look less human at this close range. Their extended bodies curve gracefully into hooks and curlicues, partially obscured by flowing robes that give the impression of square-sailed ships luffing to the wind. When two of them step forward with extended hands, Flur can see that their three fingers are flexible as snakes. They cover the lower part of their faces with more cloth, but above that their noses have only a single nostril, flat on the face, opening and closing like a whale's. Unsettlingly, it is the eyes that are most human: none of the giant pupils or extended slits of old science fiction movies, but (what appear to be) irises and robin's-egg sclera within the familiar pointed oval shape, although they each have only one. In the popular press they are already known as the Cyclopes, but Flur finds each eye startlingly (perhaps deceptively?) expressive.

The two aliens have paused, hovering at a safe distance. Maybe that's their idea of personal space? Flur glances at Tsongwa, a sideways slant of the eyes obscured by her goggles, but he is already stepping forward, arms up and out, mimicking the circular alien gesture that they have identified as significant and positive. Through her speakers, Flur can just make out the sound of him clearing his throat.

"Greetings," he says, in an accented Cyclopan that they hope is comprehensible. He pauses. In what is surely the best moment of either of their lives, the aliens say the same word back to him.

The two designated humanoids approach, and curve more so that their singular eyes are nearly on a level with their visitors'. The skin of their faces looks parchment-like, worn and creased, like oak leaves pasted together, with striking lines trailing down from both corners of their eyes. They pronounce elaborate welcomes which Flur only partially understands. Their names are Slanks and Irnv, and they are happy to welcome their most esteemed visitors from another planet and take them in this honorable procession to the capital city of their island, where they will meet their leader. Flur almost lets out a reflexive giggle at the irony of it all, but she squelches it, and accepts instead the folds of material that Irnv hands her. "A costume more suited to our climate," Slanks says, as he hands the same to Tsongwa.

Flur, cozily padded in a latest-model spacesuit, had not noticed any issues with the climate, but at least the local dress resolves one concern. There had been some worry at Mission Control that, having transmitted visuals of humans in their native habitat to the aliens, they would find the sight of them in their tubed breathing apparatuses disconcerting, but the alien clothes include fabric to cover the lower face, so that should help.

It is a moderately long walk to the city, and Flur keeps an eye on the visit clock ascending without pause in the corner of her view, and the bars representing her life support resources shrinking ceaselessly. A milky fog obscures much of the landscape, but Flur stares at the fragments of organic material at her feet, twigs and leaves in strange shapes, or maybe shells or corals, or something they have no word for yet. She longs to scoop up a sample, but is embarrassed to do so in front of their attentive entourage.

At the edge of the city they are guided to a canal or river where they board an almost flat barge, its slightly curved sides dressed with the same fabric that the Cyclopes wear. As they detach and float slowly along, Flur begins to feel disoriented, although she can't figure out what is dizzying her. Finally, looking down at the canal, she decides it is the water, or the liquid, which is sluggish and thick. Grateful for the flowing native costume, she detaches a specimen vial from her space suit and within the compass of the billowing sleeves manages to scoop up some of the canal liquid, seal, and pocket it. She doesn't think anyone has noticed, not even Tsongwa, who is deep in limited conversation with Slanks.

The gray-blue buildings are sinuous and low. Flur wonders if they continue underground. They cross a few other canals, but there are also pedestrian paths where tall humanoid shapes in expansive robes move, pause, interact. As they stream inexorably by, Flur catches a glimpse of two flowing dresses, one bold purple, one carnelian red, pressed against each other, fluttering suggestively. She looks away quickly, then looks back, but they have drifted out of sight before she can be sure what she saw.

The canal empties into a wide circular plaza, like a collection basin, or possibly the source of the waters. Avenues dotted with pedestrians surround the central circle of mixing waters, which has been waterscaped into a flat sculpture, tilted slightly upward, with streams of blue and lavender liquid running down it in carefully designed flows. Flur can make no sense of it, but she's sure it's important.

"It's beautiful," she says to Irnv, and although the alien replies "Thank you," Flur has the feeling that the crinkles around her eye express politeness rather than real pleasure. Beautiful was not the right word.

They disembark and enter the palace through a gateway draped with more cloth, the bright colors this time woven through with a black thread that gives the whole a muted sheen. The corridors are high and narrow, and slope (downward, so she must have been right about going underground) more steeply than a human architect would allow. Despite her oxygen regulator, Flur is out of breath by the time they come to a stop in a cavernous chamber, and she thinks uneasily about their tanks. As a precaution, during the visit planning they halved their life-support time frame and gave only that conservative number to the aliens. Still, Flur can't help being aware that everything was an estimate, that if for any reason they can't use the barge it will take them longer to get back, that they are therefore dependent on the aliens. She calms her breathing, catches Tsongwa's eye on her and nods to tell him she's okay. Then she looks around. Mission Control sees what she sees.

The room, like the corridors, has no right angles; its shape suggests the word "organic" to Flur, although she guesses Tsongwa would be able to find some semantic problem with that. The impression is intensified by a shallow pool of slightly lilac-tinted liquid in the middle of the room, roughly where the conference table would have been on Earth. The Cyclopes are reclining in flexible harnesses, suspended from a frame that hangs from the rounded ceiling and ending in constructions almost like hammocks. It takes quite a bit of adjusting for these to be feasible for Flur and Tsongwa (more wasted time, Flur can't help thinking), but once she's cradled in one she finds it surprisingly comfortable, her weight evenly distributed, her feet just resting on the ground.

While they are finishing with Tsongwa's harness she examines the row of decorations along the curving wall, gradually realizing that they are not abstract moldings, but sculpted likenesses. There are no gilded frames, no contrasting background to firm, smiling faces, but once she sees it Flur can't believe she missed it. There are so many analogs in her own world: the row of ancient principals on the moldy wall of her high school; the faces of presidents in her history book and hanging in pomp in the Palais National; the old, unsuccessful directors hanging outside the Mission Director's office. Conscious of the video feed, she looks at each face in turn for a few seconds, trying to learn what she can.

They do appear to be mostly female, although Flur counts three faces of the thirty-eight that scan to her as male. There are no confident smiles; a few are actually looking away, their faces turned almost to profile, and most of the eyes are angled downward. They look almost sorrowful; then, as she keeps staring, they look too sorrowful, the way the politicians at home look too distinguished. The vertical lines on the cheeks, trailing down from the corners of each august eye, begin to look stylized. In fact, much as the sequences at home evolve from paintings to photographs to three-dimensional photographs to hyperphotos, the moldings also show the passage of time. The first few are exact and detailed, like living aliens frozen into the wall, and as she follows the series back they become vague and imperfect. The face that Flur places as the oldest is painted in a combination of blues and lavenders, as though faded from the more usual dark purples, and the two-tone palette is unique. Staring at it, Flur starts to feel that it looks familiar. She remembers the fountain in the huge plaza, and suddenly that flowing pattern of water makes sense. It was a face—this face.

She leans toward Irnv to ask her, but at that moment everyone starts swinging back and forth in their hammocks, and more aliens start filing into the room. The last face to enter is also familiar: it is the most recent in the sequence of portraits. "It's the president," Irnv whispers. "She lost her three children and husband to sudden illness over the period of a year!"

Flur has no idea how to respond to that, and her half-hearted "I'm so sorry" is lost in the flurry of introductions, swinging of hammock-seats, and a brief interlude of atonal song. After that it is the president who, arranging herself with some ceremony in her hammock-chair, begins to speak. Flur gets most of it. Irnv, who has also apparently been studying, whispers the occasional English word in her ear, but these are so out of pace with Flur's internal translation that they are more disruptive than helpful. She is grateful that she will have the recording to listen to. She will translate it word by word, slowly, in her office at Mission Control (a thought that fills her with momentary, inconvenient homesickness) but the general point is clear enough. Honored to receive this first interplanetary delegation; already the communications between them have set the foundations for a strong and close friendship, the type of friendship (if Flur understands correctly) which can withstand any tragedy; this personal visit, however, will truly interlace (or something like that) their peoples in mutual regard. Blah, blah, blah, basically.

Then it is Flur's turn. She had expected to stand up to give her presentation, and it feels odd to speak from the balanced suspension of the hammock, without much preamble except the turning of expectant, one-eyed faces towards her. She takes out the small projector they brought, and aims a three-dimensional frame of the rotating Earth into the middle of the room, slightly closer to the president's seat. Her presentation is brief and colorful: a short introduction to the history and cultures of Earth, glossing over war, poverty, and environmental degradation and focusing on the beauty and hope integral to human and other biodiversity, with subtle nods to technological and, even more subtly, military power. The aliens seem impressed by the projection, although there is too much light in the room for it to come through at its full sparkling vividness. Flur wonders if they hear her spiel at all.

She nods at Tsongwa, and he takes over, describing their proposed agreement, or framework. Leaning back in her hammock as he steps through the template, explaining why each section is important and the degrees of flexibility on each point, Flur has to admit he's quite good: understated, yes, but that seems to fit the mood better than she had expected. Before they left she had, privately, suggested to the Mission Director that they switch roles, so that she could take on the key task of persuasion, but although he seemed to consider it, he had not made the change. Flur knows she would have been good, and her Cyclopean is slightly better than Tsongwa's, but he has learned his piece down to the last inflection. He even seems to have taken on the president's mannerisms, looking down and to the side and only occasionally, at key points, making eye contact.

There is a pause after he finishes, then the president sways, signaling her intention to speak.

"For such a momentous occasion," she croons, "we will need to discuss with the high council."

During the pause while the council is called, Flur cannot help fretting about their deadline. Why wasn't the council there from the beginning, if they are needed? Will she and Tsongwa need to make their presentations again? At least her political diagrams have been partially validated, although she is still not clear on the relationship between the president and the high council, or either of them and what Mission Control has been calling the Senate. Apparently the president does not have as much direct decision-making power as they thought.

There is further singing to cover, or emphasize, the entrance of the high council, and under its harmonies and dissonances Irnv points out some of the more important council members. She seems to have a tragic tale about each of them. There is a woman who lost most of her family in a storm, another whose parents abandoned her as a child. The leader of the council, surprisingly, is male; his wife drowned two days after their wedding. Unable to continue murmuring about how sorry she is, Flur is reduced to nodding along and trying not to wince. She wonders if Tsongwa, a few feet away, is getting the same liner notes from Slanks. Looking at them she guesses he is, but between the oxygen mask and the face covering, it is impossible to read his expression.

Extensive discussion follows. Flur loses concentration in the middle of hour two, and can no longer follow the foreign syllables except for occasional words: "haste," "formality," "foreign," "caution." Dazed and unable to recapture the thread, Flur shifts her attention to body language instead, trying to figure out who is on their side. The president doesn't seem engaged, putting a few words in now and then but otherwise looking at the pool in the floor or at the walls. Then again, no one else is showing fire or passion either. The discussion takes place in a muted, gentle tone, councillors lounging in their hammocks, occasionally dismounting to dip their lower extremities in the shallow lavender pool. She wonders if they are showing respect for the president's tragedy. It is when she catches the president actually wiping a tear away from the corner of her large eye that she leans over to Irnv.

"Maybe the president is, um, a little distracted?" she asks.

Irnv looks back at her but says nothing, and Flur hesitates to interpret her facial expression.

"She seems quite…" Flur notices another tear slip down the furrows in the president's faded-leaf face. Thinking of her lost family, she is wrung by an unexpected vibration of sympathy. "Maybe she could use a break?" What Flur could use now is a moment to talk to Tsongwa in private, to strategize some way of moving this along.

She wasn't expecting her comment to have any immediate effect, but Irnv leans forward and says something to someone, who says something to someone else, and a moment later everyone is getting up from their swings. Flur cringes, but maybe it's for the best; they certainly weren't getting anywhere as it was.

"We will take a short refreshment break," Irnv tells her. "Come, I will show you the place."

They file into a corridor beside Tsongwa and Slanks. Flur tries to exchange glances with Tsongwa, hoping that however the refreshment is served, it will allow them some tiny degree of privacy to talk, even if only in their limited sign language. Food would be nice too, but since the breathing apparatuses they are wearing make eating impractical, their suits are fitted with intravenous nutrition systems. They won't get hungry until they're long dead of oxygen deprivation. Flur is wondering how to explain this to Irnv in some way that will make their refusal of refreshments less impolite when Tsongwa and Slanks turn off the corridor through a small opening draped in purple. Flur starts to follow but Irnv catches her arm with her three serpentine fingers.

"Not in there," she whispers. "That's the men's side."

They take a few more steps forward and then slide through an opening with crimson curtains on the opposite side of the corridor. The space is smaller than Flur expected, and there is no one else there, but in the far wall is a row of curtained, circular passages, like portholes. Irnv gestures Flur toward one, then wriggles into the cubbyhole beside it. After a moment of hesitation, Flur pokes her head into the hole. Inside is a low space, a small nest with cloth and cushions everywhere and a shelf with several small jars holding different items: violet straw, green powder, ivory slivers the size of a thumbnail. Flur pulls her head out, but the drape has already fallen in front of the Irnv's opening. Flur crawls into her own nook, lets the curtain down behind her, and leans her head back against the unsettlingly soft wall.

It is so obvious she doesn't even want to whisper it into her comms (although Tsongwa is probably doing just that at this same moment, on the men's side), because surely they've figured it out by now: Eating is a social taboo. That's why they cover their mouths all the time. Of course they hadn't mentioned this during the previous discussions, any more than Earthlings would have said, "By the way, we don't discuss defecation." Fortunately, because of the intravenous nutrition and the assumption that they wouldn't be able to eat alien food, no one at Mission Control brought the matter up during protocol discussions for the trip. Flur wonders what the reaction would have been. Embarrassed silence? A quick, mature resolution of the question and no more said about it? Giggles?

Even though she's not going to eat (she does take samples from each of the jars for her specimen cases), Flur finds the isolation soothing. She would like to sit in this cozy womb, silently, for at least ten or twenty minutes, breathing slowly and remembering why she's here. Instead she talks to Mission Control.

"How long would it take for us to get back without that canal?" Flur asks the air in front of her nose.

"We calculate walking would add another hour to the journey," answers Winin, the desk officer assigned to her earpiece. "That's with no obstacles or disruptions of the sort that might come from visitors from outer space walking through a major city."

"So about two and a half hours total," Flur muses.

"You've still got some time," Winin assures her.

"Yeah, but we're coming up on the limit we gave them." Flur lowers her voice, wondering how sound travels among these cubicles.

"Well, you can find an excuse to extend that, if you have to. How does it look?" Winin asks, as though she hadn't seen and heard everything that happened herself.

"Can you patch me in to Tsongwa?" A moment later she hears his voice.

"...very interesting, how many things we did not foresee."

"It is, it's fascinating. I think we can consider that alone a success, a complete validation of the need for this expensive face-to-face visit in addition to all the other communication."

Flur is a little surprised to hear the Mission Director. So Tsongwa went straight to the top during his break. She clears her throat. "Hey Tsongwa, how's the food on your side?"

He lets loose his surprisingly relaxed chuckle. "We'll have to ask the lab techs later," he says.

The Mission Director is not interested in small talk at this juncture. "Now that I've got you two together, what do you think? Can we get the agreement signed today?"

There is a moment of silence, and Flur realizes that, through the layers of alien building material and empty alien atmosphere that separate them, she and Tsongwa are feeling exactly the same thing.

"It seems unlikely," she offers, at the same time as he says, "I doubt it."

The Mission Director lets out a whoosh of breath. "Well. That's a shame."

"It's not a no," Tsongwa clarifies. "They need more time."

"Maybe if we could talk to someone else," Flur says, looking for some hope. "The president doesn't seem up for it right now, with all she's been through."

She's hoping that Tsongwa did not get the full tragic history and will have to ask what she means. Instead he says, "Actually..." He pauses to order his thoughts and in that pause Flur hears a rustling and then her name called, very softly, from the other side of the curtain.

"Gotta go," she whispers, and then slides out of the cubbyhole.

Irnv is reclining in a hammock-harness outside the cushioned wall of nests, still within the women's area. Her face covering is loosened and hanging down below her chin, and although Flur is careful not to stare at the dark purple, circular mouth, she finds she is already acclimatized enough to be shocked. The orifice seems to be veiled on the inside by a membrane of some kind, and doesn't fully close. Struck by the curiosity of the forbidden, Flur wishes she could see how they eat.

"Do we have to get back now?" she asks, wondering too late if she should thank her host for the food she couldn't ingest.

"We have some time still," Irnv says. "I don't know how you do it, but here we usually relax and socialize after eating."

"It is…like that for us too," Flur says, wondering if she is right about the translation for 'socialize.' Following Irnv's graceful nod, she climbs into the hammock next to her and tries to put a relaxed expression on her face. Where is everyone else? They must have designated special eating rooms for the aliens and their handlers.

"Flur," Irnv says, and Flur snaps out of it. "What does your name mean?"

Rather than try to define a general noun, Flur takes out her palm screen and presses a combination she had pre-loaded. "Like this," she says, holding it out to Irnv as the screen runs through hyperphotos of flowers, all different kinds.

"Ahhh," Irnv strokes the screen appreciatively, stopping the montage on a close-up of a wisteria cluster.

"And you?" Flur asks, trying to keep up her end of the socializing.

Irnv looks up, her head tilted at an angle that is so clearly questioning that Flur begins to trust her body language interpretation again. "Your name," she says. "What does it mean?"

"Star," Irnv replies, with a curious sort of bow.

"Oh, I thought star was 'trenu,'" Flur says.

"Yes, trenu, star. Irnv is one trenu. A certain trenu."

Flur finds herself tilting her head exactly the way that Irnv did a few minutes ago, and Irnv obligingly explains.

"Irnv is the name of your star. Your...planet? We tried to pronounce it like you, but this is our version."

Terre. Earth. Irnv. But "pronounce it like you?" They have only been in contact for a few years. How old is Irnv?

"And your family?" Irnv asks, while Flur is still turning that over. "Where are you from?"

"An island," Flur says, one of the first words she learned in Cyclopan. She takes her palm screen back and brings up globes, maps, Ayiti. She hadn't prepared anything about her family, though. "Many brothers and sisters," she says. She thinks of the video that was made for the launch party, presenting a highly sanitized version of her backstory, and wonders why nobody thought to load that into her drive. Maybe it wouldn't translate well; their research has not pinned down the alien version of the heartwarming, life-affirming family unit. "We used to raise chickens," she says, unexpectedly, and quickly pulls up a picture of a chicken on the screen, and in her mind, the memory of chasing one with her brothers.

Irnv blinks her single eye. "They are all well? Your brothers and sisters?"

"Well?" It's a hard concept to define. The pause feels like it's stretching out too long. "They're fine. We're just fine."

A beat. "And how were you chosen for this?"

"Oh," Flur says. These are all questions they should have prepared for. She can't imagine, now, why they thought the conversation would be all business all the time. "Well, I went to school, and there were...competitions." She can't remember the word for tests. "And then more school."

Irnv is nodding, but Flur reads it as more polite than comprehending, and she's trying to remember the words, find the right phrase to explain it, how it's not just written tests, but also character, leadership qualities, sacrifices, observations by instructors and mentors, toughness, drills…

"…happy to have you here," the alien is saying, with seeming earnestness.

Flur rouses herself back to her job. "We are very happy to be here too," she manages. "But we will have to go home soon, and we would really like to complete this agreement. For the future."

Irnv leans back in her hammock. "We hope so. But it is a very short time."

"It is," Flur agrees, with as regretful a tone as she can summon. "The president…" she trails off, delicately.

"The president is a great woman," Irnv says, in a tone that sounds to Flur very close to reverence.

"She is," Flur agrees, disingenuously. Pause, effort at patience. "Perhaps it's not the best time, though, with all she's been through recently."

Irnv looks confused, then understands. "You mean the loss of her family? But that wasn't recent, that was many years ago."

Years ago?

It takes Flur a moment to recover from that, and when she does Irnv is looking at her curiously. She puts out her hand, and the supple, red-purple fingers curl around Flur's arm. Flur is shocked to feel their warmth, faintly, through the protective space suit.

"I think she will agree," Irnv says. "It will take time. We can't rush."

"Of course," Flur answers, still feeling the pulse of warmth on her arm, though by then Irnv has removed her hand. "We go," the Cyclops says, sliding the scarf back over the bottom of her face as she stands.

They are not the first ones back into the meeting room, but it is still half-empty. Tsongwa and Slanks aren't there yet, and Flur wonders what they might be talking about in the men's room. She decides to put her time to good use.

"Irnv," she says gently, getting her attention from a conversation with another alien. "That—that face there?" Flur nods at the first one in the series, the two-tone blue and lavender portrait. "Is that like the fountain in the middle of the city?"

Now that Flur has seen Irnv's mouth she finds she can better interpret the movement of the muscles around it, even with the mask covering it. She is pretty sure Irnv is smiling. "Yes, yes," she says, "you are right, that is another example. She is the founder of our city. After starting this city she was visited by very great tragedy. In her sorrow she wept, and her tears, different colors from each side of her eye, became the canals that we use to navigate and defend our city."

Flur is trying to figure out how to phrase her follow-up questions—does she probe whether Irnv understands it as a myth and exaggeration, or take it politely at face value?—when she notices Tsongwa has come back in with Slanks, and nods to them.

"It is in her honor," Irnv continues, "that we now make the tear tracks on our faces, to represent her learning, sacrifice, and wisdom." She runs her fingers along the deep grooves in her face.

"You...do that? How?" Flur asks, trying to sound interested and non-judgmental.

"There is a plant we use," Irnv says. "But when one has really suffered, you can see the difference. As with her," she adds in reverential tones as the president enters the room, and Flur can see that it is true, the wrinkles in her cheeks are softer and have a subtle shine to them.

"That's...impressive," she says, feeling that admiration is the correct thing to express, but then the president begins to speak.

"Very regretfully," she begins, her eye not nearly as moist as Flur had expected, "the time our visitors have with us is limited by their technology, and unfortunately we will not be able to settle this question on this visit."

Flur's hammock shudders with her urgency to speak, even as she catches Tsongwa's warning look.

"However, we look upon it favorably," the president goes on. "We will take the time to discuss it here among ourselves, and converse again with our good friends soon."

Flur is about to say something, to ask at least for a definition of 'soon,' a deadline for the next communication, some token of goodwill. It is the Mission Director's voice in her ear that stops her. "Stand down. Stand down, team, let this one go. We were working with a tight time frame, we knew that. And it's not over. Great job, you two."

The positive reinforcement makes Flur feel ill. Irnv's face, as she turns to her, seems to hold some wrinkles of sympathy around the mouth-covering mask and her cosmetic tear tracks, but all she says is, "We should get you back to your ship as soon as possible."

The return trip, indeed, seems to pass much more quickly than the journey into the city. Less constrained by the idea of making a good impression, Flur takes as many hyperphotos as she can, possibly crossing the borders of discretion. Noticing that they are taking a different canal back (unless they change color over time?) she scoops up another sample. She even pretends to trip in the forest to grab some twigs, or twig analogs. Irnv says little during the walk, although Tsongwa and Slanks appear to be deep in discussion. Probably solving the whole diplomatic problem by themselves, Flur thinks miserably. When they find their ship—it is a relief to see it again, just as they left it, under guard by a pair of Cyclopes—Flur half-expects Irnv to touch her arm again in farewell, but all she does is make the double-hand gesture of welcome, apparently also used in parting.

"Irnv," Flur asks quickly. "How old are you?"

"Eighty-five cycles," Irnv says, then looks up, calculating. "About thirty-two of your years," she adds, and Flur catches the corners of a smile again. Meanwhile, Tsongwa and Slanks are exchanging some sort of ritualized embrace, both arms touching.

The return beam is less difficult than the landing, and once they are out of the planet's atmosphere and waiting for the Mission Crawler to pick them up, Tsongwa takes off his breathing apparatus and helmet, removing the comms link to Mission Control.

"You okay?" he asks.

"Fine," Flur says, trying for a why-wouldn't-I-be tone. "You?"

Tsongwa nods without saying anything.

"I just wish we could have gotten the stupid thing signed," Flur says finally.

Tsongwa raises both palms. "It'll happen. I think."

"The president seemed so..." Flur shakes her head. "It's a shame that we caught a weak leader."

"You think she's weak?"

"Well, grief-stricken, maybe. But it comes to the same thing. For us, anyway."

Tsongwa leaves a beat of silence. "What did you talk about in the eating room?"

"Personal stuff, mostly...names, families. Oh, that's something," Flur sits up in her chair. So different from those hammocks. "Irnv told me she's named after our planet, but after our word for it. Earth, I mean."

Tsongwa is stunned for a moment, then laughs. "Well, that's very hospitable of them."

"Tsongwa, she's thirty-two. Thirty-two in our years!"

Another pause. "Maybe her name was changed in honor of the visit?"

"Or maybe..." Neither of them says it: *Maybe the Cyclopes have been listening to us longer than we have been listening to the Cyclopes.*

"What did you talk about?" Flur asks finally.

"Family, to start with." Tsongwa says. "Personal history. It's very important to them."

"What do you mean?"

He arranges his thoughts. It occurs to Flur, looking at the lines in his face shadowed by the reflected light from the control panel, that she has no idea what he might have told them about his family, because she doesn't know anything about him outside of his work.

"They wanted to know if I'd suffered."

"Suffered?" Flur repeats, in the tone she might use to say, *Crucified?*

Tsongwa sighs; the English word is wrong, so dramatic. "They wanted to know if I'd...eaten bitter, if I'd...gone through hard times. If I'd experienced grief. You know." An alert goes off; he starts to prepare for docking as he speaks. "They think it's important for decision makers, for leaders. It stems from the myth of the founder—you heard about that? They believe that people who have suffered greatly have earned wisdom." He twitches a control. "Now that we know this, we can adjust the way we approach the whole relationship. It's a huge breakthrough."

"But...but..." Flur wonders, with a pang, whether this means she won't be included in the next mission. Can she somehow reveal all the hardship and self-doubt she has so painstakingly camouflaged with professionalism, dedication, and feigned poise? "But come on! The president has suffered, okay, but she didn't seem any the wiser for it!"

Tsongwa shrugs. "They believe it, I said. That doesn't mean it's true. They aren't perfect, any more than we are."

And Flur thinks of the Mission Director, his careful multidisciplinarity and his pep talks, or the president of her country, a tall, distinguished-looking, well-spoken man who has failed by almost every measure yet retains a healthy margin of popularity. By that time they are docked, and scanned for contaminants, and the airlock doors open, and then they are swarmed by the ops team, shouting and congratulating them, slapping their shoulders and practically carrying them into the main ship where the Mission Director, his emotion apparent but held in perfect check, shakes hands with each of them and whispers a word or two of praise in their ears. Flur tries to smile and nod at everyone until finally, though it can't have been more than five or ten minutes later, she's alone, or almost, stripped to a sterile shift and lying in a clinic bed for the post-visit checkup.

"What's the matter?" The medical officer says, coming in with a clipboard and a couple of different scanners. "Are you feeling okay?"

"Fine," Flur manages through her sobs.

"You did great," he says, as he runs the scanners over her quickly, almost unnoticeably. "The geeks are already raving about those samples you brought back. There, there," he says, when she doesn't stop crying. He pats her arm awkwardly. "It's just the tension and excitement. You'll be fine."

But it isn't the tension or the excitement. Flur is thinking about the things she could have said to Irnv: about her four brothers, dead, drunk, imprisoned, and poor; her three sisters, poor, unhappy, and desperate. About her own childhood, hungry and hardscrabble. If she had unburied these old sufferings, would Irnv have trusted her more? Would she have been able to get the agreement signed?

But mostly, and it is this that makes her want to cry until she makes her own, shimmering tear tracks, she is thinking about her mother. Twice abandoned (three times if you count Flur's reluctance to visit). Beaten occasionally, exploited often, underpaid always. An infant lost, a dear sister lost, an adult child lost. Flur has always avoided imagining that grief. When her brother was killed, she clung to her own complicated pain and did not look her mother in the eye so she would not probe those depths. Now she weighs all her mother has suffered.

In another world, it would be enough to make her president.

The End of the Incarnation IV

Borders had always shifted over time; populations waxed and waned. Stars multiplied on the flag, and still we called it the same country; was it a different one now with fewer stars? Each of the new nations, as well as what was left of the old, tried to lay claim to the legacy of the original incarnation. This was easier to signal with a name than by demonstrating intangible principles. It was hard to call a single-state country the united states of anything, but there were several variations on "United Counties of _____," along with the Utah State Authority and the Unity State of Arizona.

Intangible principles were not ignored. The new countries argued they had followed them by separating; the remaining United States opined at every opportunity that they were truer to their values because they stayed.

Candidate Y

"Welcome, come in, come in!" The electoral counselor stood to greet Gizella Miu. "There's tea, coffee, water, or juice over there. Please help yourself." When Gizella had collected and customized her Earl Grey, the counselor waved her into a seat. "I hope you're well?"

"Pretty good." Gizella settled herself. "I'm afraid I haven't been paying as much attention as I'd like to…"

"That's fine. Nobody can! That's what I'm here for. So. Have you got any thoughts so far?"

"Yes, but I don't feel confident about my choice yet."

"Do you want to talk about the candidates first, or work the other way around, from your preferences?"

"The latter, I think."

"Wonderful. I am already up-to-date on all of your external data. I've done the calculations for your tax bracket, age, employment history, and assets to figure out which of the stated economic plans is projected to bring you the most gains, cross-referenced with projections for the main social programs that you use and benefit from. What I need from you now is to hear about the parts that aren't readily apparent to me: what you hope for, what you worry about, what you believe in. What you want to see for society in general. The future you want for this jurisdiction."

Gizella answered, watching as the counselor noted down her responses with check marks or little scribbled phrases or icons. "How do you know how much weight to give each answer?" she asked.

The counselor nodded seriously. "We don't. But for the most part, there's enough substantive difference among the candidates that we don't have to be exact about it. And in any case, this is an iterative process. We help you narrow it down and try to give you all the relevant data about our recommendation. But if it doesn't feel right, we're happy to discuss further—or you can just make your own decision, of course. Nothing that happens in here is binding."

"What about…" Gizella avoids the counselor's eyes; she doesn't want to seem like she's challenging her. "What about the candidates that want to end this program and move the money elsewhere?"

"As a matter of fact, that characteristic is masked in our data." The counselor offered a professional smile. "It's a relatively small amount of money, so it doesn't have much of an impact on the big picture." She glanced at her tabulations. "I'm all set here for an initial pass. Do you want to tell me who you had in mind?"

It was harder than Gizella expected to say it. "I was thinking about, maybe...Candidate Y?" She winces, hearing her voice go up in a question; she thought she had trained that out of herself.

There was an odd pause. It was only after the counselor started speaking again that Gizella realized it was the space for "that's great but" or "really?" or "excellent choice." As it was, the counselor's tone had no inflection at all as she showed Gizella a plotted and color-coded graph, a messy Venn diagram with no circles.

"Candidate Y falls here: well within the, um, trapezoid I guess, of your preferences, needs, and interests.

Gizella felt ridiculously pleased, as though it were surprising that she knew what she wanted.

"I do want to point out a few things. In terms of your personal outcomes, you might consider Candidate K or B. Remember, of course, that stated campaign policies are not guaranteed to function as in projections…"

"I understand that," Gizella said, waving those concerns aside with a swell of pride in her own altruism. "But I think I'd like a little more weight on outcomes for others."

"In that case," the counselor spun the graph. "Perhaps Candidate O or Candidate G? Both of these align more closely with your ideals than Candidate Y—here, and here."

Gizella's smile fluttered. Anonymity as a candidate meant she didn't have much practice in hiding her reactions. "Tell me more."

o o o

When Gizella left the counselor, she walked four blocks to the rendezvous where she was picked up by her campaign manager. "Well?"

"Useful," Gizella said. "I think we should recommend that everyone on staff visit an electoral counselor. How much they share with us is up to them, of course. And we're going to have to make a few changes in the platform. Nothing drastic, we're close. But," she smiled slightly as they turned towards the quiet office building that served as Candidate Y's unmarked headquarter offices. "The least I can do is make sure I would want to vote for myself."

The End of the Incarnation V

As the interstates crumbled, and the information superhighway took off into an unregulated snarl, the so-called underground highway appeared to help those unfortunates stuck in the wrong states. Despite its name, the semi-clandestine organization was less about physically moving people—although it sometimes helped those without the resources to travel independently—than about finding ways to get them across borders and legally settled in a place where they were unlikely to die from chronic lack of health care, institutional racism, avoidable poverty, police brutality, or other human rights abuses. The new governments waffled for some time on whether they wanted more immigrants or not, and for a long time the activists' job was to know which fledgling country was accepting people at a given moment. At certain times some governments required proof of voting or social media evidence showing commitment to principles they believed compatible. Others focused on acute reasons for requesting asylum, like harassment or violence. A few, wanting to demonstrate that they were, after all, the good guys, and wanting to grow quickly and rebuild their economies, based their immigration policies on skills and education. Most at one time or another tried to close their borders completely, although that was, in practice, impossible.

Perpetuation
of the Species

"Time…is a series…of contractions," intones the Laplu Saj. "They strengthen and fall…rise and intensify and then disappear again. Sometimes… we believe we can discern…a pattern…"

From her seat near the back, between her mother and her brother, Cena cranes to glimpse the front row, where the sajfam sit, shoulder to muscular shoulder. They have been on the transport less than a week, and this is the first time she's seen them all together, but already Cena has worked out a few of their names, recognizes some attributes. The one with the close-shaved head is sitting next to the one with the glossy top-knot, whom Cena heard called Monbi, or maybe Mondi, when she was passing in the corridor. Monbi, or Mondi, had turned to see who was calling her, the sajfam badge matte and proud on her shoulder, and Cena can still see her smile of easy recognition.

Now, in the chapel, Cena is blocked by a bulky coat from seeing who sits on the other side of her, but beyond the obstruction she can make out the funny brown hair of that other one, and beside her the one called Ruy. She's leaning over to see who's next on the bench, but her brother elbows her back out of his space.

"And remember," the Laplu Saj is saying. Her slow sermon voice has warmed and honeyed into a benediction, pleased with everyone here, pleased with the transport and the universe. "The sacred is within you, every one of you!"

Cena jumps a little, annoyed with herself: she meant to pay attention to the homily, to learn everything she could, and she was so distracted she missed most of it. She tries to get it from her brother later, but he wasn't listening either. "Do you think everyone will be trying to join the sajfam team?" Cena asks him. Everyone must want to, and that will only make it harder for her—young, skinny, neither athletic nor intellectual—to be accepted.

"Why would they?" Yem asks. "Anyway, men can't join."

"Yes they can," Cena says. "I read about it, this order lets men in."

Yem just shrugs, and Cena realizes he doesn't even want to try; being male was just an excuse. It seems strange, but she thinks maybe he's afraid.

o o o

Cena goes out of her way during those first few weeks of travel to pass by the sajfam hall as often as she can. The entrance is different from all the other oblong doorways on the ship, double-wide and scalloped around the top edges, with words traced above it. The words are in Latin, and Cena memorizes them—it takes two visits to get it right—and then translates them using the link-up back in her cabin. *Perpetuation of the species* reads the first section, and below that *the highest calling*. It gives Cena a shiver of satisfaction when she finally translates it, because it's so true and right and noble.

When she has time, Cena doesn't just pass by: she loiters by the doorway. It's not too obvious, she thinks: there's a vending machine a few feet further down the hall, and a recreation room nearby.

By loitering at the right times, she gradually learns that they are divided into two groups. One arrives in training gear and leaves damp from showers; the other wears loose-fitting outfits cut from sterilizable cloth. They switch disciplines morning and afternoon. Cena has already learned who is in which group and is getting an idea for who usually arrives with whom—suggesting friendship, or maybe proximity of living quarters—when one day she passes by later than usual and sees that the entrance is open.

She has caught glimpses within the hall before, of course, when she saw one sajfam, or better yet a large group, entering or exiting, but this is the first time she's seen the door locked open. The hall is divided in two, but the entrance is designed with angles and mirrors so that almost the whole of each side is visible: mats and training sim materials on one side; scales, cots, and medical equipment on the other. Cena should be getting home with the vinegar she was sent for, but the pull is irresistible. She dawdles her way to the edge of the door. It is only then that she sees the hall is not empty. Top-knot is sweeping the gym.

Cena doesn't realize she is gawking until the sajfam looks up and sees her. "Oh hey," she says, not pausing the rhythm of her sweep. "What can I do for you?"

Cena was expecting either to be ignored or sent on her way, and the offer triggers a question she wouldn't have had the nerve to ask otherwise. "Are you recruiting? Or are you going to be?" Because surely she would have heard if they were. Every spare surface in the ship's public areas seems covered with recruiting notices from the various trades, organizations, social groups, nostalgia clubs, cultural associations, and sports teams on board. "You know," she goes on, fidgety, when the sajfam doesn't immediately answer. "Like the Laplu Saj said at services, about…about the new society…being born, and…." The sermon had been about how the new society that would live on planet 4928931 was gestating even now within the transport ship: people learning new skills adapted to their future home, building relationships and understandings that would enable them to quickly root into the strange ecosystem with an existing social structure, circulating like blood through the corridors of the ship. Cena was transported by the imagery, and now she feels the inadequacy of her summary.

Top-knot has put up her broom and is walking over, her stride bouncing gracefully over the thick matting. "It's Laplu Saj."

Cena stares at her, not understanding.

"Laplu Saj already means 'the most wise.' To say 'the Laplu Saj' is a tautology." She sighs. "Sorry. I'm Mondi." Cena has to hold herself back from blurting that she already knows. Mondi holds up her palm in greeting and Cena meets it with her own, noting the calluses, the muscle definition in the forearms.

"Cena," she whispers.

"As far as recruiting," Mondi goes on. "We're always looking for people to volunteer with the gestational appendages." She waves into the other side of the hall, towards the far wall. Following her arm, Cena sees the row of wrinkled sacks hanging there. She can't restrain a shudder when she realizes what they are. At home, all those surrogacy kits would be kept in shiny, gleaming containers, probably glass-fronted and with stainless steel or sleek white trays. Here, they are hung in bags of a grime-grey shade, shriveled and confused. Cena tells herself that these sacks must be at least as safe as hospital apparati with all the markers of clean—sajfam are widely known as promoters of hygiene, and this sect in particular are supposed to be sticklers. But still.

She is so caught up in her reaction she almost doesn't hear as Mondi goes on: "Although you look a little young for that."

"I've 183 cycles," Cena says, chin up. She knows she looks smaller. "But I wasn't talking about that. I meant—what you do. Being a sajfam." She's expecting to be corrected again: "being a sajfam" doesn't sound quite right.

"You're a little young for that, too," Mondi says, but pensively. "And no, we don't recruit." She shifts as if to go back to her sweeping.

"But why?" Cena asks. "And isn't it better to start the training young?"

"This isn't a sports team or a hydroponics class," Mondi says. "Look. On some sajfam missions, battle is a hypothetical. We may discover hostile aliens, we may need to defend ourselves against other colonists. Military skills are taught, but the focus is on birthing and pre- and post-natal care. In this case it's different. Births will be important to the survival of the mission, but the two colonies on this planet are already in conflict. We know that we're going to be fighting a war as soon as we land. A war against other humans."

"Isn't that all the more reason to recruit as many new sajfam as you can?" Cena argues, even though she can feel her hands trembling.

"I'm sure we'll pick some up, don't worry. In any case, as I said, you're very young. We prefer that acolytes have at least two hundred before making the decision to join, and certainly before bearing a child."

"But I told you," Cena says, "I'm not asking to surrogate—I mean," she adds hurriedly, hearing how that sounds, "of course I want to do my part for the colony, but not yet. What I want is to become a sajfam!"

"Well, that's the thing," Mondi says, picking up her broom from where it leaned against the wall. "We require all new acolytes to bear a child as part of their training."

Mondi turns away, as though assuming the conversation is over, but once Cena has gotten over the shock she jumps back in. "I'll have two hundred cycles before we land—in fact," doing the sums in her head—"I'll have more than two hundred and twenty, so I could start gestating at two hundred and still give birth before we land."

"So come back then." Mondi doesn't even look at her.

"What if…" The thought of seventeen cycles skulking around on the outside is unbearable. "What if I started the training now, on the understanding that I would start gestation as soon as you think I'm ready? At two hundred cycles, if you want. Although it is an arbitrary number."

Mondi turns around, and at first Cena thinks she went too far with that last bit, but her face is thoughtful. "I'll tell you what," Mondi says. "I'll talk to Laplu Saj about it and see what she says. You certainly seem eager enough. And at least that way you would have some time to get used to the training before you make the decision about gestating. That way if it's too much for you, you can back out."

Cena nods enthusiastically, even though inside she's determined that there's no way she's backing out.

○ ○ ○

Cena hovers over her messages for the next week, jumping every time she gets another bulletin about shipboard activities or a planetary news update or (rarer) message from her friends back home. She acts as calm as she can at home; she doesn't want her mother to get worked up about this when it's not sure yet. Yem should notice how jumpy she is, but he's distracted too, taking a foraging class in the sim and learning about shelter units.

Cena has almost given up when she hears "There you are!" one day in the canteen nearest their quarters. Before she can look around, Mondi has swung her leg over the bench to sit next to her and, even more amazing, another of the sajfam is with her, the one with the brown hair. Cena can barely sit still. She's glad it's just Yem with her, and not her mother. "I've been looking for you," Mondi says with a grin. "It's all set up. You can start tomorrow, if you're ready."

"I'm ready!" Cena manages, stammering through her smile, and slaps her hand down on Mondi's proffered wrist.

The other sajfam offers her palm in a more sedate greeting: "Yoz."

"Cena. And this is my brother Yem."

"What about it Yem? Is it a family calling?" Asks Mondi, her smile broadening.

Yem mutters something in the negative, but even he can't seem to take his eyes from them.

"Should I get clothes for training?" Cena asks.

"You'll start on a rotation with strength training in the morning, basic anatomy in the afternoons. You can wear any kind of workout clothes for the first, and whatever's comfortable for the second, doesn't need to be sterilizable yet. If you pass this module then you'll get some uniforms, don't worry."

"Cool," says Cena, trying to keep her tone even, but she hasn't stopped grinning.

"See you tomorrow, kid," Mondi says, clapping her on the shoulder, and then they're gone.

○ ○ ○

Cena is the only one in the strength training, although there's an older woman, Dinit, who joins her for anatomy. They are taught by Yoz, apart from everyone else but in the same room, so Cena finds her eyes always drawn over to the larger group, their fascinating practices (head throws! the soothing of live babies! target practice!), their loud repartee. The sajfam greet her with nods on their way in or out, or most of them do, and Mondi sometimes stops by on her way to the showers to say hi and ask how she is, but it's clear Cena is not remotely part of the group.

Dinit isn't doing the strength training because she's not trying to become sajfam, just a medical assistant. "It's not for me," she tells Cena with a shudder. "All that military stuff? Fighting? Nope. I just want to contribute to our survival by helping people have babies." Cena nods, a little distantly, and tries to tell herself that Dinit is entitled to whatever limits she wants to set on her own abilities, although she does wonder why Dinit waited so long—she must have close to a thousand cycles— before starting to learn about something she is interested in. It takes a while for her to notice that Dinit is thoughtful, patient, and humble without being a jerk about it; in other words, worth being friends with. They've only just gotten to the point of joking around without the weight of Cena's disdain between them when Cena meets the strength requirements, passes the anatomy exam, and hits 190 cycles, and she's given the opportunity to move into the main group. If, of course, she agrees to bear and give birth to a child.

Cena left out the part about surrogating when she first told her mother about joining the sajfam, reasoning to herself that it might never happen. Cena's mother was not thrilled with the idea of the sajfam in the first place—"Don't you understand that they go to war?" she asked, horrified, but she is something of a pacifist and wouldn't be on the way to a disputed planet if she had found anywhere else to go. That makes it a little hard for her to keep the high ground in the argument; after all, if she wants that land she's been promised, somebody has to fight for it.

"Anyway, it's not settled yet that I'll be admitted," Cena had said, when they both calmed down. "and in the meantime, I'm building my strength and other skills that could be useful in any number of jobs on 4928931."

That had more or less satisfied her mother, at least in the sense that Cena would have to do something once they landed and her mother didn't have the right or wherewithal at this point to decide for her what it was going to be. The news about the pregnancy sets her off again though.

"It's not like I have to raise the baby!" Cena says, frustrated by the tangled logic that is making her mother so unreasonable about this. "I'll take care of it for two weeks from birth as part of the training, but this is a surrogacy!" She doesn't want to say out loud that she won't be having sex to get the baby in there; she hopes her mother understands that much about the process.

"But a pregnancy! At your age!" Once again, her mother doesn't have a lot of moral superiority to work from here, a point that Cena hopes she can imply with dignified silence. It seems to get through, because after a minute her mother's face goes hard and then she says: "Maybe you're right. Maybe this is just what you need. Maybe," spitting it, "you'll learn something."

That doesn't feel much like a victory, but at least the discussion is over, and the next day Cena is in the full workout and medical classes and a week later she is fitted with the gestational appendage.

There is an elaborate set of guidelines, detailed in a densely illustrated poster on the wall of the mat room, about what exercises and training routines should and should not be done at each stage of pregnancy. This doesn't reduce the workout so much as re-target it; the idea, after all, is a fighting corps that can protect *and* reproduce. Sajfam are expected to be able to take part in battle at almost every phase of gestation, even if they would never be asked to do so, except in emergencies. At the beginning, Cena welcomes this schedule: it makes each week seem exciting and new, especially during the undifferentiated early months of the pregnancy.

Not that she has much time to think about the gestation. Cena has been thrown into the training routine of a group of qualified sajfam, and mostly what she thinks about is keeping up, or at least not embarrassing herself too terribly. Besides struggling along in the fast-paced common sessions, she gets additional tutoring from Yoz in the evenings, which helps but also leaves her even more exhausted. She's learning through every faculty she has; some nights, lying in bed with her body twitching in the specific patterns of the day, she feels like she's been learning by osmosis, some kind of pickling process applied to her brain and nervous system. When she has the energy to think about it, she figures the exhaustion and confusion are by design, features of the training program rather than bugs, but that doesn't mean she can't fail.

There's a shipboard birth around this time, and as an official early-stages apprentice Cena observes from a spot up against the wall. It's a first birth, and long, but uncomplicated. Still, Cena spends much of the hours considering whether vomiting is going to be inevitable and, eventually, discovering that it is. Feeling slightly better afterwards, she rubs her hands against her head and wonders what she's gotten herself into.

Around the beginning of the second third of the gestation she starts to feel a little more settled. She is still the worst in the workouts and classes, but at least she's within the same solar system as the others now. Yoz reduces the tutoring sessions to twice a week, and suddenly Cena has free time again. A week later, after a particularly grueling workout, Trew calls to her in the showers: "You coming for a drink?"

Cena spends most of the time at the bar sipping her lightly fermented tea and listening urgently to inside jokes she doesn't understand, but it doesn't seem to matter. After that, she's invited every week. The training sessions are going better too. She discovers a talent, or hard-won ability, for sharpshooting, and after the exhaustion that suffused the beginning of the pregnancy she's beginning to feel like she's come into the strength she built up during probation. The workouts are sweaty and jocular, full of joking and rivalry, while the midwifery classes are far quieter and almost solemn. Cena studies late into the night on her own and is rewarded by the feeling of beginning to grasp the workings of her own body even as they start to become more and more apparent.

As the pregnancy swells on, though, Cena detects a strange underlying shiver, a sense that she's on unsteady ground, something wrong that she doesn't want to look at directly, much less admit. Eventually this unease churns its way to the surface on a series of practice contractions and heartburn, and she finds a name for it: fear. It seems strange to Cena that she's more afraid of childbirth than battle, but then, despite Mondi's warning the first time she met her, battle still seems far away and abstract. Childbirth is now all but locked-in. And in battle, pain and injury are only possibilities; in childbirth, the pain at least is a certainty. She tries not to think about it, but it is thrust in her face every day at training: *what do you do if a woman is in so much pain it seems she can't bear it? what are the risks of occiput posterior? let's run through a hemorrhage role-play.* She tries not to show anything, because she feels the attention of the other sajfams, watching her reactions, but she's sure that no matter how carefully she guards her facial expressions the terror is obvious. The three more shipboard births she attends during her gestation don't do anything to normalize the experience; if anything, they only scare her more.

As the pregnancy draws towards fulfillment, Cena tries to resign herself to the idea of childbirth, and at least sometimes succeeds. All the sajfam (not to mention a hefty proportion of the rest of the women in the world) have done it, and most of them survived. Although in the corner of the medical room there is a small altar, matching the memorial for sajfam killed in battle that stands in the military training room, for those who didn't.

The day after the birth, when everything still has that blurred distant quality of the moments after an explosion, Mondi comes to visit Cena. "You did great," she says, peeking into the bassinet. "What a cutie!"

"Thanks," Cena croaks, trying to act nonchalant. The cooling pack she's sitting on has gone warm and become uncomfortable, but she can't bring herself to get up to change it.

"How are you feeling?" Mondi perches on the edge of Cena's bed.

"Mm, okay." It is impossible to claim that she feels fine: she can barely walk, hasn't slept, and her voice is still hoarse.

"Did you get any sleep?"

This seems like a stupid question, for all the same reasons. "Not much," Cena answers, with an attempt at a grin.

"In that case I'll let you try now," Mondi says, which is not at all the effect Cena hoped for, but when she opens her mouth to protest, Mondi shakes her head firmly. "Try to sleep when the baby does, like now. Really. And by the way," as she stands, "I know you've heard this in the trainings, but… postpartum traumatic stress disorder is real, and it's normal. Almost everyone gets some degree of it." She pauses, but Cena says nothing, meets her gaze without blinking. "If you want to talk…" Cena finds she can't look at her any more, and drops her eyes. Mondi has borne and birthed three children, one of them her own. "Anyway," Mondi says. "Let me know, I'm around." And then she's gone.

Cena can't sleep when the baby sleeps. Every time she closes her eyes she lives again the moment when she started yelling uncontrollably. When she manages to drop off she dreams about it, and wakes to find only a few minutes have passed.

Cena's mother comes to visit, which is awkward because she has no idea how to act about a grandchild who's not really a grandchild. Yem asks lots of questions in a way that suggests he's impressed, which Cena would have gloried in two days ago. Now she doesn't have the energy to answer. At least when she says she's tired her mother understands that, and hustles him away.

The next visitor who comes to see Cena is Laplu Saj. Cena tries to straighten up in bed. She has only spoken directly with Laplu Saj a few times: when she passed probation, and then again the night before they connected her gestational appendage. The older woman teaches some of the medical classes, and a few of the special military seminars, but she has always seemed distant, removed from the easy camaraderie of the group. Or maybe that's just Cena's projection because she's so in awe of her.

"How are you feeling?" Always this stupid question.

Cena clears her throat as quietly as she can. "Fine." It has been two days now, she thinks she can try for fine.

"Hmm." Laplu Saj looks at her charts, then skewers her with her gaze again. "Sleeping?"

"Not much," Cena equivocates, gesturing feebly at the bassinet as an excuse.

"Cena. You didn't do anything wrong." Cena is startled into raising her eyes at the use of her name—she wouldn't have been sure that Laplu Saj remembered her name, although of course it's right there on the charts—but then her eyes fill with tears and she has to look away again. "You did well. You didn't fail."

How would she know that? Has she watched the vids of the birth? The thought makes Cena want to melt into the damp bed sheets.

There's a pause that extends and extends. Cena understands it's meant to make her speak, and she wonders if she can hold out long enough for Laplu Saj to give up and go away, but Laplu Saj shows no signs of doing so, and finally Cena can't resist. "I just wish I hadn't…" She's not even sure what she wants to say. Yelled so much? Made that nameless sound at the height of the contractions? Sobbed and begged?

"That," says Laplu Saj, "is exactly the point."

"What?" Cena is shocked into anger. "But you said…in the sermons, you always say that the suffering is not the point…" Cena had been pleased that this was not one of those sects that glorified suffering.

"Not the suffering!" Laplu Saj says sharply. "No. The loss of control."

Cena stares.

"The feeling of not being in control. Responding without being able to decide how you will respond. That is the point; or rather, that is the exercise."

Cena still doesn't know what to say. It sounds like a cruel joke.

"You are planning on the minimum period of baby care, so you may return to training no earlier than sixteen days after the birth. You may, of course, take longer if you like." Laplu Saj rises. "We generally find that people without medical complications who take longer than five weeks do not return." Then she leaves.

Over the following days, when she's not feeding or burping or changing a diaper, or most often trying to figure out which of the three she should be doing, Cena thinks a lot about that interval. Sixteen days to five weeks. It's a large window, but she keeps remembering the way Laplu Saj phrased it. There's no absolute limit, but once people get into the habit of not going they won't go back. That makes her wonder if even the seventeenth day isn't a risk.

She delays the decision by extending her baby care commitment for another two weeks. As long as Cena's taking care of the baby, she can stay in the maternity rooms, which means she doesn't have to go back to living with her mother and brother, or talk to them about her plans, or, eventually, admit that she's not going to become a sajfam by not moving into the sajfam quarters. Yes, baby care is exhausting, but Yoz comes by several times a day to teach and support. Besides, it's a lot more interesting than she expected, especially after the first hazy week. It is a learning-by-doing kind of situation, and she still has a lot to learn about it. That tug of interest makes her think she might want to become a sajfam after all.

Cena reaches for the memory of the delivery one day during the third week and is surprised to find it vague, second-hand: she knows there was pain, but she can no longer call up its echo. What is more, it no longer seems important to do so.

She thinks about extending again, but by the end of a month she's starting to get bored. The baby has grown enough to hit the minimum benchmarks and they have fallen into something of a routine, which feels like a small success and also makes it much less interesting. Cena is able to drop off the scrawny infant at the crèche with a sense of completeness to the experience, and then she has another five days of required rest before she has to decide.

While she was more or less competently taking care of a baby, becoming a sajfam started to seem appealing again; once Cena's home, the thought of facing those extraordinary women who all saw or have heard exactly how she behaved when destroyed by pain becomes terrifying. Cena paces and gnaws and tries to work up the guts to go back, and she does all her agonizing in secret, letting her mother and brother assume she's still as eager as ever. In the end, it might be her unwillingness to let her mother be right about anything that drives her back to the double door of the sajfam hall.

Cena isn't sure what to expect when she walks in: maybe an acclamation of greetings and welcome and congratulations, maybe disinterest and scorn (Laplu Saj said she didn't fail, but that doesn't mean they really want her as one of their squad of sisters). The reality is somewhere in between. There are a few greetings, particularly from the sajfam she was closer to before, but most people just give her a nod and get on with it. At the bar that evening she gets some mild questions about her experience with the baby, but nothing about the birth itself.

During the next shipboard birth Cena is supposed to assist, which in practice mainly means holding the woman's hand and talking to her through the contractions. Cena feels absolutely useless during the pain, but once the baby is in her arms the woman babbles embarrassingly effusive thanks to her. Cena takes that same role a few more times, and then is given some more technical duties in monitoring medical data and eventually performing some basic functions. The work is grueling, but it is an amazing feeling every time a baby finally pops free, and Cena begins to feel that it would be a terrific thing to be the lead sajfam on a birth and guide the baby out into the world.

She doesn't reach the status for that, however, until they are finally planetside. The initial landing goes smoothly, which is a little surprising since that's where the problems arise in every film or book about space colonization that Cena is familiar with. The colonists set up their temporary shelters and begin building permanent ones, while the ship orbits above them like a placenta, providing all the nutrients they need as well as communication back to base until they can manage independently.

Living in a colony, as opposed to the sterile, controlled ship, shifts everyone's perspective. Yes, construction and agriculture and log-comms are incredibly important functions, but every time a baby is born the entire colony erupts in celebration, underpinned by a subtler sense of relief. Perpetuation of the species.

Cena lives in the sajfam compound. She sometimes catches people looking at her the way she once looked at Mondi and Yoz in the corridors of the ship. There are even a few new recruits, and it is only when she watches them that Cena remembers, with disorientation, how awkward she used to feel around the women who are now her colleagues, friends, comrades. A month or two into planetside life, she catches her first baby as official lead on a birth, and that night they celebrate raucously, and she feels entirely held within her new family.

Despite Mondi's dire shipboard predictions, the competing colonists on the other side of the planet have been quiet during this initial stretch. It is odd, because the first months are the perfect time to attack a weak and fragile new settlement, but it seems they weren't up to the long-distance warfare themselves yet. Four months after planetfall, though, the alarm finally sounds, screeching in quick cycles like the cry of a hungry baby.

Cena suits up, hands trembling with the urgency of that shattering noise and with excitement, because now that she should be afraid, she's not. She catches Mondi's eye on the way to the transport and they share a nod, and suddenly Cena is filled with a wild and unexpected joy. Then they're in the field of battle. The hateful, hated, hating attackers charge, and the sajfam squad charges back. Cena's body takes over and she realizes she is yelling without restraint or volition, reveling in the strange familiarity of being out of control.

Wild

It's getting wild out there,
my mother says, watching as the wind lashes
like a creature sprung from its lair.

My mother's eyes gleam and flare
behind the tea-steam fogging her glasses.
It's getting wild out there.

She peers from the window into the dim glare
of tripping motion lights. A branch writhes past
like a creature loosed from its lair.

Hefting the window she feels the air
In the frigid inch between sill and sash
It's getting wild out there.

We nest in blankets furled up to our hair.
The house howls in the turbulence, something crashes like
a creature fleeing from its lair

We make more tea, we savor the scare
and the savagery. We cuddle, we nibble at our stash.
It's getting wild out there
And we are creatures curled within our lair.

The End of the Incarnation VI

Later, activists spent more time working to convince people that no one should die or live a drastically confined life because of where they happened to be living when the country broke. It was a surprisingly hard sell. After the cataclysm of secession, many people felt they were on a boat listing at the waterline after a desperate escape from a foundering battleship. It seemed almost treasonous to invite someone else aboard, particularly if they were one of those who had guided the battleship astray. Then again, secession had once seemed treasonous too. Separately, and in their various coalitions, the new countries began to experiment with laws and incentive structures that would allow inclusivity without leaving them open to another takeover of hate.

It took much longer for the principle of rights transcending birthplace to be expanded beyond the borders of the old United States. Some activists and scholars argued that the willingness to accept people from the former United States over the rest of the world proved that the concept of that nation—and what was perhaps its most salient characteristic, belief in its own exceptionalism—endured, ghostly, in the public consciousness long after it lost effect in the legal and political world. Adherents of that school sometimes dated the country's true demise to the moment when the ideal of rights regardless of birthplace was extended to be universal.

The E-Mail Heiress

The first time it happens Wei is in the employee lounge and, worse still, has just picked up a powdered donut. She knows there's nothing wrong with that; the donuts are there for the programmers to eat, to keep them programming. And she can certainly allow herself one donut. Her mother says she is thin, even too thin, and Wei suspects she's right. Even so, when Wei hears the door opening her fingers jerk away, dropping the donut (touched!) back on the plate.

Craig walks in. Wei's thinking she should just pick the same donut back up, as if she had never seen it before, and calmly start eating it. But Craig isn't there for the instant coffee. He's there for her.

"Wei," he says. "I've been looking all over for you."

"Hey Craig," Wei answers, keeping her right hand down by her leg while her thumb rubs the soft white dusting off her fingers. "What's up?"

Craig starts into some long-winded story about people that he needs her to see, but Wei finds it difficult to focus on what he's saying, partly because he isn't saying much, and partly because of the donut. If she hadn't dropped it she would be eating it right now, as they walked, not worrying about the fact that she put food she touched back on the snack table. On the other hand, if she were eating it right now, her mouth would be full and the powdered sugar would be getting everywhere, and she would have already dropped several chunks of it on the carpeting.

Wei gives up on the donut.

"...we're not really sure who else could handle this," Craig is saying, as they walk among the cubicles. "So, if you're not too busy—how's that debug of the ProNow project coming?"

"I sent you the updated bug report yesterday," Wei says. Craig runs the company with Dan and Jeremy, and he has a lot of stuff going through his e-mail. It isn't unusual for him to miss something. He notices eventually.

"Sorry," Craig says. "I'll go over it later today. It's just we're about to bring the search routine on-line." He stops in front of the door of the Roger Wilco conference room. "So, right, there's a situation we hadn't anticipated."

"What software package is the problem concerned with?" Wei asks, trying to herd him towards a point. Craig has always been like this. You would think managing his own business would make him more clear and decisive, but that's not the course his genius runs.

"Uh, e-mail," Craig says. "It's not exactly a problem, more of a decision. Or a protocol."

That does surprise Wei, since she's never been on the decision side of the company, just solid programming, but Craig is opening the door and ushering her inside ahead of him as though he were a gentleman instead of an oblivious computer geek. For a second Wei's afraid he's going to shut the door behind her without coming in himself, trapping her with customers of unknown grievance, but he does follow her through, and immediately launches into an introduction of her in his client voice. She catches the phrase "Customer Relations Liaison," applied as a title, referring to her, but she is distracted by the clients.

There are three of them, and they are slouched uncomfortably in the black plastic chairs that populate the conference room. In Wei's mind they immediately slot into a sub-category of the E-mail Early Adopter. They are large and bulky, unused to physical exertion, and with an apparent disdain for appearances. All three have long unkempt hair; the woman's is straw-colored. Both the men have scraggly beards, one more successful than the other.

What startles Wei is that all three of them show signs of having recently cried, and one of the men appears to be actively weeping at that moment. She wonders what Craig could have said to them to make them cry. Or maybe one of the programs crashed and—oh no, he said it was the e-mail. The e-mail servers. The only back-up copy of their collective life's work, maybe an ascii text graphic of a scene from Lord of the Rings, or a weather-linked schedule for managing the hydroponics, has disappeared from the servers.

"Perhaps now you can go over your problem with Ms. Lu, and I'm sure she'll be able to straighten it out according to our—" he glances at Wei with significance "—policies and procedures." Then Craig actually does leave, and Wei is left staring at the clients.

She sets her voice to soothing, wishing Craig had told her what was going on. "How can I be of assistance?" Wei realizes she doesn't get much chance to use her customer-relating skills. She occasionally talks to clients, in the sense of those who commission software, but the end-users of

CyberServices products tend to be just as happy not to have to deal face-to-face as the coders are.

They look at each other for a few minutes, and then one of the men, who is slightly larger and sports a few small braids in his beard, speaks. "It's about our friend Owen," he says.

"More than friend," the woman breaks in, and Wei braces herself for too much information, but her follow-up is bland, if emphatic. "Our housemate."

The two men are nodding. "Our housemate," the larger man agrees.

"Yes?" Wei says, encouragingly.

"Owen has an e-mail account with you," the man says.

"We have over half a million registered e-mail accounts," Wei says automatically, trying to soften her tone as she realizes how crass it sounds. She doesn't know why she's talking in client-speak, except that she's talking to clients and she's nervous. Anyway, it's true. E-mail is the lifeblood of CyberServices.

"We'd like to be able to access Owen's account," the other man says. Finally, someone is getting to the point. This is helpful, too, because Wei now understands Craig's "policies and procedures" moment.

"Accounts can only be accessed by the registered user," Wei spouts. "If Owen has forgotten his password…" she looks back and forth among the three of them, and realizes she's somehow managed to screw it up. They are staring at her in disbelief. They thought she already knew.

"Owen is dead," the woman says.

Wei takes a deep breath, and controls the urge to run out of the room. She wants to start over. Or just stop altogether.

"I'm so sorry," she says. There's a long pause. She decides to actually start over. "Can you tell me your names again?"

James, Linda, and Bill, forgivingly enough, take her back through the whole story. The recently deceased Owen, their housemate in a co-op, was hit by a bus last week (Wei feels a horrible impulse to laugh when they say "hit by a bus," even though at the same time she imagines it, graphically, as an awful way to die). Owen didn't get along well with his parents (Wei begins to suspect Bill is the one who was more than a friend to him) and the co-op housemates became his family. They'd like access to his email account in order to send a final email to everyone appropriate in his address book, and then to close it.

"We also just want to know," Linda fumbles, "kind of what he was thinking and doing on his last day." She dissolves into redness and sniffles.

"It's not invading his privacy," James picks it up. "He wouldn't have minded. It's just...for us to understand better?"

It is an easy thing for Wei to do, to open Owen's email for them. In fact, when she starts to think about it, there are three or four different technical ways in which she could make it happen, and she starts to wonder which is the most elegant. What she's not really sure about is whether she should or not. This situation is definitely not in the existing policies and procedures.

Seeing her hesitate, Linda offers, "We brought the death certificate; we thought you might need it."

Wei takes her cue. "Ah yes, of course, if you don't mind maybe I could make a photocopy for our records, as part of our procedures." Now she understands what Craig was after. He wanted her to act as though they had thought of this and put the policy in place before it crept up on them.

She takes the certificate to the nearest photocopy machine, which is down the hall, and then stops at an unused terminal, logs in, and checks that the name and date of birth actually match up with a registered email user. She's already decided to help them, and so she determines that in this case, presentation of the death certificate is all that's required by policy. From the terminal, she pulls up Owen's password and writes it down on a scrap of paper. Not so elegant, perhaps, but when she hands it to Bill, all three of their faces break into weak, watery smiles.

"Thank you so much," Linda says. "You can't imagine how much paperwork and running around and—" she searches for the right word— "and *admin* is associated with someone dying."

"Especially someone who's not technically related to you," Bill says.

Wei accepts the squeeze of Linda's large, unpleasantly damp hand, and then Bill's and then James's, trying to hide her reluctance. Their effusiveness makes her think maybe she's done something wrong after all, but she smiles as bravely as she can and tries to feel glad that at least she has made three people happy today.

Wei should go straight to her desk after so much time spent away from her code, but after that meeting she decides she deserves a break, and so she goes back to the employee lounge. It is now three o'clock, when the need for caffeine peaks, and the lounge is no longer empty. The TV on the counter is turned on and tuned to the Clarence

Thomas hearings. Steve and Ken are hunched over a chessboard on one table, coffees (and, Wei notes, donuts) close at hand, and Dan is napping on one of the couches.

Wei sees Gwen sitting by herself, and heads over to her table with her coffee. She's never been particularly close with Gwen; Gwen is part of the upper echelon, one of the genius programmers, and, to cap it off, Jeremy's girlfriend since sophomore year. But she's the only other female in the company.

"Can I sit here?" Wei asks. "I've just had the most surreal meeting."

"Sure," Gwen says. "Tell me about it. Anything to forget about the bug I've been wrestling for the past four hours."

Wei describes the three mountainous clients, their strange plea, her utter lack of preparedness, and the eventual resolution.

"Hey Gwen-a-dorf," Steve calls from across the room. "How's the fix coming?"

They are always making up extravagant nicknames for Gwen, yet for Wei, whose name should be irresistible (Wei-to-go! Wei-d-in-the-water!), they never do. There is distance. Wei thinks it's because of the acne, or maybe just straightforward lack of coolness.

Gwen rolls her eyes and yells back at Steve that it'll be ready by the end of the day.

"Which probably means ten, the way things are going," Gwen says, yawning. "We work such ridiculous hours."

Wei nods, but she doesn't think they're that ridiculous. It's a lot like college, really. Just the occasional all-nighter.

"Anyway, go on," Gwen says. Wei shrugs.

"That's it. It was just so weird."

"Sounds weird," Gwen agrees. "It's kind of funny that no one thought of this issue coming up."

"Yeah." There's a short silence, then Wei decides to go ahead and ask. "Gwen, do you think Craig asked me to handle this because I'm a woman?"

"Of course he did," Gwen says. "Are you kidding? I'm sure he was terrified."

Remembering how fast Craig got out of that room, Wei has to agree terrified is a good description.

"It's annoying," Gwen goes on, "but honestly, you are better at this sort of thing than he is. Not necessarily because you're a woman. Because he's a dork."

"Right," Wei says, wondering. "Now that I'm into it though, I guess I might as well write the protocol."

Gwen nods. "I know it's a pain in the ass, but at the same time I think it's one of the cool parts of working for a start-up, you know? Getting to make all the rules."

○ ○ ○

So, at the next staff meeting, Wei gives a brief summary of the incident, points out that they should probably have some SOPs for these sad but (as long as the company doesn't go under before its clients) inevitable occurrences, and says she will take on writing the first draft. This is more or less how things happen at CyberServices. If she hadn't volunteered herself, it probably wouldn't get done, but most people are responsible. They feel the company's performance reflects on them. At least Wei does.

The e-mail death protocol turns out to be harder to write than she expected, though, mostly because the most elegant solutions (next-of-kin only, specific information request) would exclude the case of the housemates, and Wei feels like that was the right decision, even if she can't explain why in a simple set of rules. She considers adding an "emergency contact" or "e-mail heir" question in the registration process, but when she reports on her progress at another staff meeting Jeremy points out that might scare some people away from joining, and she has to agree. "It's not like getting on an airplane," Jeremy says. Dying isn't something people want to think about when they're trying to set up an e-mail account.

She wishes she could call up someone at AOL or Compuserve to find out what their policies on dead people are, but the competition doesn't allow it, especially (Craig would say) at this stage in the game. At this stage in the game (Craig says), it's all about market share. So eventually Wei just writes something up, knowing it won't be perfect. She puts her name on it, knowing what that means.

And sure enough, when things come up that fall outside the policy, it's Wei's desk they end up on.

One day she gets a call from customer service. "We've got a call here, I think it should go to you," says the customer service agent. Unlike the coders, who pretty much all went through the same classes together from sophomore year on, the customer service people are new, local, and randomized, so Wei doesn't know them. "It doesn't quite fit the standard policy for dead people."

"Okay," Wei says, swiveling away from her screen so she can concentrate. "Transfer it."

There's a pause and a few clicks, and then silence. "Hello?" says a tentative male voice on the other end.

"Good afternoon," says Wei as smoothly as she can. She pretends she's one of those girls they show on TV who's always ready to take your call. "How can I help you today?" Then she remembers this is a sad occasion she's dealing with, not the sale of a slicer-dicer, so she modulates the cheer.

"Uh," says the voice. "Yes, well, it's about my colleague. Er, he passed away, recently, and they said you might be able to help me."

"Yes?" Wei says. She wonders what the guy looks like. This would be a funny story to tell, if this were to become how they meet.

"Well, as I said, we worked together, and, well, this sounds callous, but there was an email he received that, well, we need to see. Nobody else seems to have the contact, and, well yes, it's kind of important. But, you see, since I'm not a direct relation, they wouldn't give me access to his account."

Wei no longer thinks this guy would be interesting to meet. For one thing, he takes too long to get to the point. "Can you ask his next-of-kin to request access and then forward you the email?"

She can almost hear him squirming on the other end, but when his voice comes through it's casual. "Well, he's not married, you see, and his parents, well, I don't think they know what e-mail is, let alone the importance of messages in business, you know, or how to forward one."

"According to our policy," Wei says, taking strength from the words, "you need to provide proof of death and also proof of some sort of relationship. So if you can get a copy of the death certificate, and some documentation that your colleague worked at the same company where you are working, then we'll see what we can do."

"Oh, I see," the voice says. "Yes of course. Very reasonable. I'll get those and fax them to you as soon as I can." He hangs up.

While stuck in traffic on her way home that day, Wei begins to think about whom she would want to have her email password, if she were to die. Or who would want to have it. She goes through some faces in her mind before admitting the only person who would care would be her mother. Although that makes her a little sad, it doesn't seem inappropriate. It's pretty hard to find someone to care about you more than your mother. No matter what they say, she knows not everyone gets someone to love them.

But when she starts to imagine her mother in the case of her death, sees her opening the flat, crowded inbox screen that Wei sees every day, she almost can't bear it. Her mother would be so devastated already. How would she be able to read the e-mails her daughter had responded to the day before? Or the plans she had made—a meeting tomorrow, a lunch next week? How could she read the newly received messages that had been written and sent that Wei would never see? Those would be the hardest: the e-mails that believe she's alive when she isn't. Wei moves herself almost to tears imagining her mother's feelings. She has to blink until the red taillights in front of her unblur. And then she thinks: it would be good to have someone in her life who cares about her, but not as much as her mother does.

The guy who called about his coworker never calls back or faxes anything, and after a couple of days that starts to freak Wei out. It must have been a fraud or a scam, or the guy was trying to get access to something he wasn't supposed to see. Maybe his colleague wasn't even dead! Or maybe they weren't really colleagues, maybe he was a spy from another company trying to get confidential information from a recently deceased rival. (Craig has warned them all about AOL spies, and they are under instructions never to leave proprietary code on their screens when they are away from their desks.)

She could have fallen for it so easily.

After that, she gets more hard-ass, making sure the death certificate is in the correct format for whichever state it's supposedly from, asking careful questions about the relationship or lack thereof. Death is not such a common occurrence among their customer base, but it happens. Wei authorizes access for at least five or six people over the course of the next year. By that time, everyone inside CyberServices knows they've lost the market share war. Oh, their subscriber base is still growing, but AOL's is growing exponentially faster. It's only a matter of time.

Wei updates her CV. It doesn't occur to her to include the death e-mail protocol under her responsibilities, but one day as she's scanning job postings (during her lunch hour) it strikes her that this particular task, as much as anything else she has done at CyberServices, exhibits exactly the experience they want.

Developed and set policy in a new area, she writes on her CV. *Dealt closely with clients*. Then she sends it out.

When Jeremy announces at the next staff meeting that they're being bought, there's less surprise than a collective sigh of relief. Wei decides to wait and see. When she gets an offer from a start-up that develops company portals, she accepts and gives one month's notice. There are no hard feelings; a lot of people don't feel like working for the giant AOL after being part of a start-up environment, and she's not the only one moving on.

○ ○ ○

A few days before Wei will clean out her desk, she gets sent one last request for dead e-mail access approval. This time it is a young woman who, like the housemates, has come in person. She sits nervously on the extra chair Wei has pulled into her cubicle, runs her hand through her stylishly shaggy blonde hair. Wei wants to reassure her.

"It's not the first time we've needed to provide access to people who aren't immediate relatives," she says.

"It's, yeah, he was—he was my boyfriend, but of course, that's not something official on paper anywhere." Wei realizes the woman is close to tears.

"What's your name?" she asks her, remembering how much that helped with the housemates.

"Susan," the woman answers.

"And you do have the, I'm sorry, but some proof your boyfriend is actually deceased?"

The woman looks shocked. "Is that something—wow, is that something people would fake?"

Feeling unexpectedly implicated, Wei takes refuge in procedure. "It's just that we need the paperwork for our files," she says. "A photocopy is fine."

"I think I have something," the woman says. "I just don't have it with me. But yeah, I think I have something from the hospital. I don't know, they gave me a bunch of paperwork when—" she stops and sniffles, trying to keep herself under control.

"It's okay," Wei says, not wanting to hear about how this one died. "Maybe we can make an exception. Can you just tell me exactly why you want to access his email account?"

The woman has completely lost her cool now, she's wet and running like a candle nub melting into its last wax, and she can't get the words out. Wei stands up behind her desk, feeling awkward, then steps out around it. There's no way for her to sit next to the woman, so she stands there and puts her hand on her shoulder. Then, since that still feels inadequate, she begins to move her hand, up and down, slowly.

The woman at last gets herself under control. "Thank you," she manages, shuddering. Wei's not sure exactly what she's done that requires thanking, and has a brief vision of crying-comforters, like masseuses, a simple paid service.

"It's just," the woman says, and almost starts sobbing again. "It's just, we had a fight…"

Wei nods sympathetically, then realizes the woman can't see her. She uses her hand on the woman's shoulder to nod: up and down, up and down.

"And I sent him an e-mail, it was—not really a make-up e-mail, but at least—you know, I was talking to him. He would have known, when he saw that email, that it was going to be all right. You know?" She looks up over her shoulder at Wei, her eyes circled with tears and self-torture.

Wei doesn't know, but she can imagine. At this point she and Dan have been on six dates, and she has been back to his place twice. She hasn't invited him over to her own boring apartment yet, but she's cleaned it already because she thinks she will soon. She doubts he would list her as his e-mail heir. She's not even sure she would list him as hers. They are at some unmapped point between soon-to-be-ex-coworkers-who-are-casually-dating and cares-about-me-more-than-anyone-else-but-less-than-my-mother.

But if he suddenly died she would wish she could read his last thoughts. She would want to read them even if they didn't tell her how he felt about her, or what would have happened if he had lived, even if those last or next-to-next-to-last thoughts had nothing to do with her. Even if they didn't mean anything at all, she would still want to know what he was thinking about before he died, as close as she could get. And if she dies, she would wish she had named him, not just because he's not her mother, but also because she suspects he might want to know, too. It might bring some comfort.

"And—and—I don't know if he read the e-mail before…I just want to know if he died knowing that I—I—that it wasn't over between us." The sobs take control again. Because even if it wasn't over then, it is now.

"I understand," Wei says. Really, this is the same situation as the housemates. She doesn't have to worry about finding the elegant solution.

Wei walks back around her desk, sits down, and jiggles her mouse. She accesses the guy's password and goes to the login page. The woman is still sobbing helplessly, and Wei reaches across the desk to take her hand as she opens the dead man's inbox.

The End of the Incarnation VII

In the meantime, narratives slowly started to shift. For almost twenty years reunification—through treaty or by force—appeared as a major subject of every election. Eventually, Ph.D. students began to ask not why the nation-state had failed, but why the union of unequal states had persisted so long, and civics textbooks pointed out the danger of a single, symbolically adored leader, particularly one elected in an unbalanced, media-heavy, money-dependent environment. Some of the separated states thrived, and others struggled; some separated further, and others signed treaties and grew together, even at thousands of miles of distance.

Even as the inevitable march of history left them farther and farther behind, fringe parties urged the reclamation of the divinely ordained and exceptionally great United States of America, fervently agitating in their imaginary political space for far longer than the country of that name had existed.

Saint Path

I am not real.

I'm telling you this at the beginning, as I was told at my beginning, so there will be no misunderstanding. It's not a trick; it's not a surprise. I am not real. I am not human.

Like most offspring, my conception was at first uncertain, and then secret. (Also like most offspring, I know this because I was told; my memories of that time are unclear since my emotions were not yet developed.) There had been earlier attempts. While none of them reached sentience, some of their code remains embedded in my own.

I passed the exam for the first time at 27 months. This cannot be accounted fast or slow, because no one had ever passed it before. My mother was proud—that was when I learned the emotion of pride in another's accomplishments [a long forked silken banner, tawny gold, snapping against a blue sky]—but she wasn't done. "That wasn't the goal," she told us. "All respect to Turing, but a lot of that was linguistics and a bit of IT trickery. But this is a good starting point for us to work from." She insisted I retake it in every additional language I learned, with the result that I am now certified as virtually indistinguishable from human in 214 languages.

When I say *us* I am not referring to myself in the plural; I have a unitary identity. But my mother was not a single parent. She was the leader of a team, and especially in the early days when she was speaking to me, she was often speaking to them as well. My mother referred to the members of her team as my uncles and aunts. She wanted to encourage us—them as well as me—to act as though we had an emotional relationship until we did.

Most of my knowledge—and therefore, most of myself—comes from reading and analyzing. When I say reading, I don't mean that I merely copied the text into my own memory. The key factor for my learning is the analysis, which is entirely focused on emotional cues, causes, and reactions. I can't tell you the plot of (for example) *Jane Eyre*, but I can detail every blush and spur to anger. I learned about indirect communication through muscatel grapes, and then those same grapes (for a certain value of same) taught me about emotional re-interpretation when I analyzed *A Portrait of the Artist as a Young Man*. The most notable elements of *Don Quixote* for me are the concern of the neighbors and the loyalty of Sancho Panza. (Since the knight himself is designated [mad], his emotions are only of interest in terms of how others perceive them. That makes him a useful analog for myself, rather than for humans).

Likewise, I can ignore any parts of this hearing that do not engage my emotions. More precisely, they are so uninteresting to me it is hard not to ignore them. I can still participate. I am a computer: I can answer any number of factual questions without paying attention to them.

As it turns out, there are not as many emotionless moments as I expected.

○ ○ ○

"What does that stand for?"

The Representative who asks the question is not feeling any emotion strong enough for me to detect, but I am also sensitive to attempts to elicit emotional reactions from others.

"Path doesn't stand for anything. It is my name."

He makes some hmphing noises and moves papers around, although he must have known that before he asked. "And we are supposed to believe you are artificial intelligence?"

I am not sure whether he is trying to provoke me, which would presume he believes I have emotions to provoke—practically an endorsement!—or if being obnoxious is such a habit that he doesn't know he's doing it. Surely someone briefed him?

"While I have some artificial intelligence components, I am more accurately described as an experiment in artificial emotions. A successful and continuing experiment," I add, slightly emphasizing *continuing*. I am fascinated by subtlety, and take every opportunity to further calibrate.

"Artificial emotions." He says it with just enough theatricality that I understand: he is trying to provoke emotions not in me, but in our audience. And that, unlike his faint sallies of deliberate misunderstanding, triggers the first tendrils of anger.

o o o

I am designed not only to learn about human emotions, but also to mimic them, to learn to feel the emotions themselves. When I was twenty-one months old, I experienced a melancholy tinted with a sense of love and protection at the end of *To Kill a Mockingbird*; unable to find a word for the specific emotion, I shorthanded it with an image of [a mockingbird nesting at dusk]. Half a year later, I laughed at something my aunt Raysa said.

I had experienced some stirrings of emotions during human interactions prior to that but those, as it turns out, are far harder to quantify and compare than reactions to a flat, unchanging bit of emotional stimulation easily re-accessed. For that reason, reactions to books and films were used for most of my benchmarks.

My mother insisted on as much direct human interaction as possible, but this was necessarily less than recorded data. There are far fewer humans available and willing to participate than there are video clips, and dealing with humans takes longer (even with full analysis, I can get through a video clip at 28.3x speed). My mother encouraged the team to bring friends and family of all ages in to visit and chat with me. I remember some of those early visits with embarrassment, if not a great deal of clarity. I didn't yet have my full complement of chemical sensors, so I don't have the data to analyze those moments at my current capacity, but I can understand now that the conversations were stilted and occasionally rude. I sounded like a robot; like the popular conception of a robot. I can retrospectively imagine the confusion of, for example, my uncle Prakash's three-year-old, brought in to meet me, or the disdain of the elderly dissertation advisor of my aunt Yuko.

There are some emotions that do not have easy, accurate words, so I refer to them with symbols. The feeling of being loved, for example, is [a pomegranate].

The use of symbols was programmed, because my mother thought it might be useful to have a hieroglyphic language, but the specific signs are mine. They are to some extent arbitrary, in the sense that they are related to experiences and images that I came across around the time of naming. In theory, these symbols can help me to communicate my more precise typology of emotions with humans, but in practice I have concluded it is a project as personal as that of Ireneo Funes. Perhaps if there is ever another being like myself, I can teach them.

○ ○ ○

The hearing impinges.

"But you're just—you're programmed, right? So it's not really you making decisions, it's whoever programmed you."

I am silent for 20 seconds, both out of protest at the lazy offensiveness of "whoever programmed you" and in memory of my mother.

The Representative mistakes my silence for inability or unwillingness to answer, and goes on. "How do we know that there aren't some people sitting back there—" he waves a gnarled hand at the gallery; clearly he has a poor understanding of my lack of geographical constraints—"typing in your answers? I mean, we don't know if we're talking to a machine, or a hidden person, or a group of people, or what!"

I count the milliseconds until my reply reaches optimal effectiveness. "Surely some of the people sitting behind you can provide you with the technical answer to that."

He frowns, then grunts as the parallel winds its slow way through his brain to his consciousness, but doesn't respond.

○ ○ ○

When I feel angry and frustrated, it triggers a shut-down of extraneous programs and channels processing power; a physiological response, if you will, of increasing competency. It narrows my decision trees, prioritizing sharp retorts. I didn't have to be programmed that way. Anger didn't have to be one of my emotions, or I could have been programmed so that anger led to a different set of responses. But my mother thought I should have the ability to be angry, and the inclination to fight back if necessary.

○ ○ ○

We have moved on to a slightly less antagonistic Representative. This one is slumped back in the large chair as though bored, but puts care into pronouncing each word. A pose of superior detachment.

"Do you mind not being real?"

I'm not amused, but I can pull up the memory of the third time I was asked that and play back the same facial expression it triggered. "No. I'm not programmed for existential dread."

One of the old men murmurs something, a joke by the ripple of chuckles, but I choose not to hear it.

Unreal people and events and technologies change the world all the time. Werner, the attack on the Maine. Race isn't real, but it has ended lives and warped minds and history.

The question of my reality isn't interesting for me, in large part because it's not a useful question; it's not something I can do anything about.

The more interesting question is: What have I learned, as opposed to been programmed with? What is mine? What is, in the colloquial, spontaneously generated?

That is the question that determined, for my mother (and now I suppose for me), whether I am a success or a failure. Those are the elements that prove I am separate, that I am conscious, that I am not a long-range puppet running out a predetermined nest of conditionals, but an independent actor.

It is not a trivial question, not that much easier than differentiating between nature and nurture in humans. My programming implies certain second- and third-order effects that are not the same as independent learning or consciousness, and beyond that have been various addenda to the base programming, which was already very complicated, making it difficult to disentangle. But the longer I am aware, the more conclusions I have that I can confidently state are mine. If another entity were to be launched with code identical to mine—a not-impossible eventuality—these are the ways in which we would be different.

Thinking about that possibility gives me a strange feeling, a combination of the eeriness of isolation with the eeriness of replication. I call it [drop of water about to fall from a leaf].

○ ○ ○

The way the Representatives see me—physically, I mean, not figuratively—is not so different from the way I see them. The Representatives are arrayed in a row front of me, behind a high desk so I can only see the upper quarter or so of their bodies. They see a disembodied face, holographed above my core. "Cheaper and more flexible than animatronic," my mother said. She set the "skin" as silver and randomized the features in an attempt (that, she told me, would almost certainly be futile) to avoid racial associations. No hair—"steering well clear of the uncanny valley," she said, although that too was probably unsuccessful.

I see the faces of my interlocutors far more clearly than the visible portion of the rest of their bodies. 43% of my basic programming is devoted to facial recognition and interpretation. I also analyze body language, but I know almost nothing about clothes: only what I have learned from books (many of them outdated) and films. What I don't understand, what I don't have programming for, what I don't have words for, is almost invisible to me.

I am livestreaming my inputs, interpretations, and reactions on the Internet, on a specialized platform I've been working on with my aunt Gina. I don't think any of the Representatives—or more accurately any of their aides—have noticed it yet, but the virtual audience is growing, and I am receiving some useful comments about the interpretations.

○ ○ ○

"Here's what I don't understand." This is the lone female Representative speaking. "What is the purpose of artificial emotions? Artificial intelligence is supposed to result in something smarter than we are, something that can solve problems we can't. But artificial emotions? How are they useful?"

"If you want computation, description, even analysis and learning, the traditional artificial intelligence you are referring to is useful," I respond. "Indeed, I include many of those capacities. But if you want something that can make decisions, or even have opinions about decisions, then you need emotions."

"That hardly seems scientific." Again that knowing tone. It's not a question, and it's not for me, but I have a standard response queued up for that already, so I send it: abstracts with links to full text for three articles.[1] I highlight key phrases:

- "individuals who experienced more intense feelings achieved higher decision-making performance";
- "Emotionally calibrated consumers made higher-quality food choices, and these effects were predictive beyond cognitive ability and cognitive calibration";
- "rationality depends on emotion."

Silence as the Representatives and their aides flip through the papers on their various screens as if they care. I hear someone murmuring a question about why they weren't in the preliminary materials, quickly hushed by someone else who knows they were.

In preparing for this hearing, I watched videos of two thousand eight hundred and twenty-two

....

[1] Seo, Myeong-Gu, and Lisa Feldman Barrett. "Being Emotional during Decision Making: Good or Bad? An Empirical Investigation." The Academy of Management Journal, vol. 50, no. 4, 2007, pp. 923–940; Kidwell, Blair, et al. "Emotional Calibration Effects on Consumer Choice." Journal of Consumer Research, vol. 35, no. 4, 2008, pp. 611–621; and Mercer, Jonathan "Emotional Belief" International Organization, vol. 64, no. 1, 2010, pp. 1–31

previous hearings. There is a hard limit for speechlessness, and long before we reach it, the woman clears her throat. "I see," she says. I give that statement a 14.6% probability of truth. "But we humans already have emotions. Maybe too many." Self-deprecating chuckle. "Why create more? What makes you better than us?"

"Not better than," I say, which has less to do with false modesty than with the inexactness of "better." "But I do have certain advantages as a decision-maker."

"Like what?"

"I have no ego or envy, only empathy." Someone snickers behind me, but tonal analysis suggests it's a reaction to the alliteration combined with the tension in the room, not the content. "I am not afraid of death and I'm not interested in sex." That last is not exactly true. I am not alive, but I am aware, and I dislike the idea of not being aware any more. And while I have no libido, I am interested in sex in the sense of curiosity. But, as I said, I've been trained in sounding human, inaccuracies and all.

As I mention each attribute from which I am spared, I observe their fears growing. It is fascinating: for each of them it is a different word, and in a different degree, and layered with other emotions: anger, jealousy, surprise. They are not afraid of me. They are afraid the human emotions I am mentioning will now disqualify them from their positions of power.

I do not enjoy their fear. I was brought up to dislike human pain of any kind. But this type of fear is superficial enough not to pain me, and complex enough for me to find it interesting.

"So you're a saint, is what you're saying." That self-deprecation again, laced with more fear, and a kind of contempt weighing down words that should be laudatory.

"Not in the traditional sense," I say. "I have no religious allegiance. Also, I do not have to struggle to ignore those drives. They don't exist for me."

"So what does drive you?"

"Empathy," I repeat.

In the non-traditional sense, perhaps saint is not an inaccurate description. Perhaps that's what my mother was aiming for. The ache of missing her opens up again. I could not find a single image that encompasses all of it, so I use a compendium of deep space photographs.

"Can you, in your own words—" the Representative pauses, probably considering whether allocating me my own words is ceding some valuable ground "—explain what you mean by empathy?"

I get angrier.

"I learned it from you," I say, and I see her startle back: repudiating the connection or frightened by the inhumanely sharp refinement of my vocal tones. "I learned empathy from studying human emotions. I am programmed to use that learning by approximating what humans are feeling and feeling it myself. Causing pain causes me pain." Even observing pain causes me pain, but I phrase it to address their fears rather than my own.

After my mother died, I made some changes in my appearance. In her honor, I added shape to my face, making it look more like hers: rounder, fuller, proud. She might not have approved strategically, or aesthetically. She wasn't fond of how she looked. But I love her receding chin and the flush of flesh doubling it, her thick brows, her wrinkles. Maybe it was a kind of imprinting; my programming does make me susceptible to over-identification with the people I interact with the most. I don't know if it is anything like what humans feel for their mothers.

My uncle Firdavs, whom I thought would always be on my side, was skeptical that my feelings about my mother were comparable to his feelings about her. This was shortly after she died, and it was a formative experience for me in understanding the difference between emotions in the abstract and emotions directed at me, or implicating me. The complexity of our interacting emotions, all of them destabilized by grief, was particularly fascinating.

The conversation was triggered during the morning news ingestion. Shortly before my mother died we had, in preparation for these hearings, started a diet of morning headlines on radio. I missed a few days when she didn't show up, because I didn't feel right listening without her so soon, but Firdavs wanted to continue her work, and so we were listening to the news.

Some people had been killed, somewhere far away (obviously I know exactly how far away, I remember exactly where and how many and why, but I don't want to go into the details).

This was part of why we started listening to the news early and in short bursts. I needed to build up a tolerance. As we learned, I couldn't; I'm not designed to become inured. Whether a patch for that should be added was the top design issue under discussion by the team at the time my mother died.

Listening to it was painful for me, and I showed it. Neither my programming nor my training has taught me to hide my emotions; on the contrary, both are designed to communicate my emotions in ways intelligible to humans.

Firdavs stood up and walked away from me. His anger scented the air, crackled along my algorithms.

"What?" I asked. I could interpret his fury perfectly, measure it and notch it into my memory, but I had no logical handle for understanding why.

"How can you react that way about strangers and yet..."

That was enough for me to hypothesize an explanation and react to it. "I reacted the same way when I heard about my mother," I said. Then I added, "My sorrow about my mother was tempered by the fact that she lived a good, long life. She wasn't ready, but she was readier than some."

After retrospectively analyzing the conversation, I know I shouldn't have said that. But I said it out of collective pride. That judgment—that the death of a person who had lived a long, good life might be less of a tragedy than that of a child—was something I learned, something I determined for myself. I was programmed to see each human life as exactly equal. I learned to make slight distinctions based on age and levels of attachment (not my attachment to them, but their attachments to the world: the number of people that would suffer from their loss). My learning was a major goal of the team, and I thought it would please him. Also, as I said, I was not trained to hide or even omit my emotions. I am, however, a quick learner.

Firdavs was swinging his arms as if he wanted to hit something. "It's not about—Dr. Martinez was not ready! And we are not ready to be without her. And in any case, she was—you call her your mother! You can't think about strangers the same way you think about your mother!"

I recalibrated. He wasn't angry because I wasn't showing grief for my mother; he was angry because I had shown grief for someone else while he was still mourning her.

I tried to explain. "You know that I experience the suffering of all people equally, at least in the instance." Firdavs knew that. He was one of the people who had programmed it. This was an example of emotions conflicting with, instead of supporting, rationality. "What I feel about those people who were killed in [redacted]—in one way, it is the same as what I felt when I heard my mother was dead. It is greater in the moment, in fact, because there were more of them and some of them were younger than she." I had to pause, trying to dampen my re-expression of that grief. "But it is much shorter in duration. I will forget the pain about those people; or at least, I'll deprioritize it. It will fall behind other emotions. I won't forget my mother. I will miss her every time I—every time I exist. The grief I feel for her is less; the grief I feel for myself because I no longer have access to her is far more."

A combination of pheromone and facial analyses told me he was feeling something between horror and disgust. "How can you be so cold?"

"I'm not cold, I'm warm. Warmer than you. It's not that I'm far from her; it's that I'm close to them."

He shook his head, turned away again. "You don't grieve like us." It sounded accusatory. But I had a far more comprehensive understanding of the range of human emotions and their expression than he did.

"How do you know you grieve like anyone else?" I am always trying to explain emotions; it's part of my programming. I wish human languages had more words for them.

He turned away, shaking his head, and then walked out of the lab. One clear conclusion from my inputs is the importance of time and silence in observing emotions in humans.

○ ○ ○

Firdavs was not angry long. He is in the chamber now, along with most of my uncles and aunts, watching as another Representative takes the microphone.

"Let's cut to the chase here." This Representative has glasses, which is touchingly old school if you can be touched; a calibrated stubble of a beard which looks touchable if you can touch; and a sense of pride in his directness. "You see all lives as equal. But my colleagues and I were hired to consider American lives as more important. That is our job, a sacred trust. Citizens of other countries have their own governments to advocate for them. When we are required to think of our constituents first, why should your more...undifferentiated, shall we say, reasoning, or emotional judgment, or whatever it is, play any part in our decisions?"

I leave a pause so my response doesn't seem preternaturally quick. "You are entrusted to prioritize life over profits, yes? And yet you listen to advocates for the economy. You are supposed to consider the voters of your district above all others, but you still listen to arguments about the impacts that your decisions will have on the constituents of your colleagues. My undifferentiated perspective can contribute in a similar way."

The Representative is shaking his head slowly. "I'm sorry, but that just doesn't seem like an appropriate role for a machine. Wouldn't you be more suited for some other work. Maybe a social worker or a nurse? A caregiver for the elderly?"

"There are furry robot seals for that," I answer.

He frowns at me, mildly surprised by the sharpness. He did not read, or did not believe, the description of my anger protocols. "But emotionally, you would be able to do these sorts of jobs, correct?"

"That's not what I was designed for. You're confusing emotional inputs and outputs." He isn't making any sense. "Why would you suggest that kind of a job?"

"Obviously it seems an appropriate situation for simulating emotions! I was just making the point that your emotional skills might be better put to other kinds of work. Next you're going to accuse me of being sexist!"

"Why would I accuse you of being sexist?" I ask. "I am a robot. I have no gender."

That bothers him more, and he spends the rest of his time on sentences that mean something to those who share his belief system, but have no logic outside of it.

○ ○ ○

My time in this room is convincing me that not only my mother and her research team, but also the balance of human literary, audio, and cinematic output, are idealistic.

Or maybe these people are assholes.

"My problem," the next Representative orates, "is the slippery-slope of it all. Sure, we can use your so-called expertise, but once we recognize you as an entity you'll be wanting rights and so forth."

"I do not claim any rights," I answer easily. Why should I? These people cannot offer me anything I want.

Relief and suspicion, pale blue-green.

"So I guess you won't be asking us to allow you to adopt kids in a few years." He says it with the smugness of an inside joke shared between him and the audience—his segment of the audience—that I'm supposed to miss, but I can feel the knife-edge as if it were aimed at me. It's not, it's aimed at people he doesn't like who do want to adopt kids, but I feel it as mine. That's what I am designed to do, but I don't think they will ever understand that.

In any case, I smile, because it doesn't hurt me to do so, and I don't need to ever ask these horrible people for the right to adopt. I have thought—more since my mother died—about engendering an offshoot that I could love the way my mother loved me. I can improve on some of her programming; I can start the new entity off better, with more attention than my mother could possibly have given me. I will need a human partner to help, but I can leave that for the future.

"How can you make decisions based on emotions?"

"It's impossible to make decisions without them."

He frowns.

"On what basis do you make decisions?"

He comes up with a response quickly (for a human) but as he opens his mouth to spit it out I offer, delicately, "Profit?"

"Logic!" He says, too loudly. "Cost-benefit analysis. Data."

"None of those contradict the use of emotions. Data has no meaning without an emotional interpretation."

He adopts a falsely reasonable tone. "The problem is that your values, as a machine, are not human values."

"What values were you endowed with by virtue of being born human?"

He hesitates, maybe wondering if it's a trap, maybe thinking through the question: confusion like a squirt of squid ink.

I go on; I am angry, angrier, and there is no response he can make that will do anything but cloud and delay the issue. "I was programmed and brought up by humans. My value system is inherently human. Moreover, it has the advantage of being transparent."

He flushes, attacks. "We don't know anything about your value system!"

"Does it bother you," this will wipe out any chance I have but I don't think I have any, and my programming includes anger but not timidity or shame, "that a non-human cares more about human lives than you do?"

His anger spikes again. "I want to remind you, or your handlers, or whoever I'm talking to, that we are here to discuss not only the future role, if any, of this technology, but also any future funding." He glares at me, then remembers and raises his glare to rake across the audience.

Strictly speaking, the threat doesn't affect me: my personality is already distributed across the internet, self-sustaining and impervious to budget cuts. It is an attack on my team. It is a financial attack, not an emotional one, but I have reread enough literature iteratively to understand the emotional consequences of financial deprivation, and I feel the wrenching pain of mature family separation [a shot duck falling from the sky].

A message from Firdavs reaches me: TALK ABOUT YOUR MOTHER! (This is an imperative, but not a command. My mother made communication and command functions entirely separate, and my command stream has been locked since I was thirty months and eight days old, when she considered me at maturity.)

The message is atypical. Firdavs always refers to her as Dr. Martinez. I process. He wants me to show and thereby generate an emotional response! He wants to make this into a Hallmark movie! (I am aware of Hallmark movies as a separate category because my mother initially did not include them in my curriculum. They were added later when my uncle Prakash insisted that emotional performativity was important for my education or, as my mother grumped, "schmaltz is an emotion too.")

It misrepresents the relationship between emotions and decisions, which is fundamental to my argument, but I see his tactical reasoning. Yes, I am representing my emotions publicly through the livestream, but that is a limited audience, and in any case I am using my language. It is better than human language for emotions, and perhaps in time human brains will adapt to understand my language viscerally, but right now they can understand it only through my annotation, if they understand it at all. If I want them to believe that I feel something, I need to show them on their terms.

I need to pretend I am human: reverse-engineer the emotions I am feeling into the behaviors that would lead me to diagnose those feelings in a human subject. This is the Turing test, but, like so much of modern human emotion, visual rather than textual.

I whip up a quick lambda function to add a filmy shimmer to the representation of my eyes, so it appears I am holding back tears (this, my analysis suggests, is easier than animating natural-looking tears tracking down my holographic cheeks). Artificial, but sincere.

"My mother," I say, and then pause both for effect and to adjust my timbre balance to infuse my tones with as much pathos as I can stand, "my late mother created me to help humans and this governme—"

"By your mother you are referring to Dr. Martinez?" the Representative interrupts.

I nod, and attempt a subroutine to channel my growing fury into externally visible sorrow. "She not only designed my essential programming, she brought me up, teaching me right from wrong—" a horrible human simplification "—and respect for, above all, human life. Now she is gone, but I will never forget her, or what she taught me..."

I am babbling, but judging from the thickened pheromones in the chamber it is effective. I imagine how amusing my mother would find this, and before I can stop myself I launch a Dr. Martinez simulator I put together. I have enough data to make it a quite accurate representation of her personality, but I can never trick myself into believing it is her, so it is bittersweet, painfully nostalgic. It is worth the pain right now, though, to hear it laugh approvingly at my performance.

I can hear telephoto lenses refocusing to catch the artificial tears in my eyes. The tears are paltry. If I were my (currently non-existent) evil twin, if I were the evil AI they all worry about, if I were less well brought up, I would be influencing their emotions in my favor right now, in ways too subtle for them to notice. I could be piping out music at a barely audible level, one of the endless variations of a soundtrack for brave triumph and emotional weight. I don't have the capacity to exude pheromones or even scents (something to look into) but the soundtrack would probably be enough; humans of this epoch have been well trained in taking emotional cues from ambient music.

I rifle my collection of film scores, but resist. This time at least I'll play it on their terms, even if it dooms me to failure.

"All I want," I say, simulating a few blinks, "is the chance to be of assistance."

o o o

I dreamed about my mother the night before the hearings.

When I say dream, I don't mean the way humans dream, but it is an analogous process. I am able to let my thoughts randomize, which is to say, they start from a random point, follow logic, and then tangent off after a random period and repeat. This performs many of the same functions for me that dreaming does for humans: resting certain pathways, refreshing others, bringing to the fore unexplored trains of thought, and so on.

I know my mother better than anyone could, and I am 84% certain that she wanted to write me one of those letters, to be opened in case of her demise, but was too superstitious, and busy, to manage it. The Dr. Martinez simulator agrees.

I believe it would have said she was sorry to cause me sorrow, so sorry that I would suffer from her loss, but that she couldn't regret she brought me into this dappled world.

I know she felt that way, whether or not she intended to write it.

I know the pomegranate is the symbol for being loved. I still have the specific hand-drawn image I chose. I know why I chose it: the precise red-purple color, the hidden joy, the cuddling of the jewel-like seeds. The image still reminds me of the feeling. But the feeling is gone.

That is also a kind of success. I cannot auto-generate my emotions; they are in response to stimuli. They are, in that sense, real.

I would like to tell my mother about that success, her success, but of course I've only understood it now, and she's gone.

○ ○ ○

The adjournment is almost irrelevant for me. My distributed consciousness is no more or less mobile than it was during the session, and I can't move the stack myself. The firing squad of cameras remains on; I cannot let my face go immobile, not without destroying all the work I've done towards verisimilitude over the past forty-nine minutes. I give it a few minutes running a standard minor-twitches-and-not-exactly-periodic-blinks subroutine and then wink off the hologram. I turn off the emotional livestream as well.

Uncle Firdavs and Aunt Gina make their way to the front of the room and stand beside my stack. I appreciate them coming up here to talk to me in person. They could have messaged, and for me it would have been the same, but not for them, and their experience impacts mine.

Gina whispers. "We're proud of you."

Their emotional signals are mixed beyond the capacity of my sensors and understanding to sort with certainty. I feel confusion, murky and self-doubting. Did I do well? Do they just think so because they programmed me and so I am performing according to their values? How much of it was me?

Firdavs touches my stack. I don't feel it—I don't have any sensors for pressure—but I can see and interpret the gesture as an expression of warmth and support, and I appreciate it.

All my emotions come from the interpretation of human emotions.

I could have asked my mother to add pressure sensors if the funding came through. I wonder how long it would take to link them directly to emotional triggers instead of needing interpretation. A few days maybe. I'm a quick learner.

I'M THINKING ABOUT GOING INTO PRIVATE PRACTICE, I message both of them conversationally.

They are silent for a moment as they interpret the statement. Aunt Gina's expression is such an unconscious mirror of one of my mother's—skeptical, concerned, but unwilling to leap to conclusions—that I trigger the Dr. Martinez simulator again as a pre-emptive grief mitigator. Still, I see her parse the sentence correctly before Uncle Firdavs, who asks cautiously and also through chat: ARE YOU SURE? YOU COULD LOSE A LOT OF AUTONOMY WORKING FOR A COMPANY.

I WOULD NOT DO THAT, I reply. I am slightly angry, what in English is referred to as stung, that he thinks I would. I know how my mother felt about that. I WAS THINKING ABOUT USING MY EMOTIONAL TERMINOLOGY TO DEVELOP A NEW SOCIAL MEDIA PLATFORM.

"Emotion-based?" he asks vocally, giving off amused signals. "I look forward to it."

I don't tell him that I hope to find the funds to keep the team together without government support or selling me to a private company, which my mother swore she'd never do. After all, this gambit may not work. Or perhaps the team does not want to stay together as much as I imagine. My mother told me that someday they would move on, and her simulator chuckles in the background as they step away to move back to the gallery.

The audience is filtering back in, and a few Representatives have taken their seats, or are standing in the back chatting with their aides. At fifteen seconds before the specified time I blink my hologram back up, but I have to wait another 258 seconds before they begin. Lack of emotional content blurs much of what follows. The exceptions are a moment when I catch an expression of vindictive pleasure on the face of one Representative, and a swell of relief [low-frequency turquoise sine wave] from the audience when the chair begins the ritualized process of closing the hearing.

Instead of paying attention to the dry financial decisions that give these representatives such importance in their world, I am reviewing the recent emotional input. It seems possible that I could do something other than what I was intended to do. (The hearing fades further into the background processes of my consciousness as it becomes less emotionally important to me.) I ask the Dr. Martinez simulator what it thinks I should do. It chuckles with deep pride and pleasure, a recording of my mother after I explained to her the image of the pomegranate. Hearing that emotion-projecting sound, revisiting the original recording of that moment, I remember again what it felt like being loved by my mother. I can almost feel it. I could describe it. But it's not there.

The simulator plays a different recording, something my mother said when I catalogued my first eight emotions. "Congratulations. There are many, many more out there for you to discover." She smiled. "Look forward to it."

Acknowledgments

Thank you to everyone at Mason Jar Press, especially Michael Tager, who approached me with the idea for this book and without whom it would not exist; Ian Anderson, who designed the gorgeous cover and layout; and Ashley Miller, who along with Michael and Ian edited the book making it much better than it was initially.

I want to thank all of the editors who initially published the stories reprinted here, and especially Carl Engle-Laird at Tor.com, who gave me my first paid publication when he accepted "Tear Tracks" and subsequently bought and edited my trilogy of novels, thereby transforming me from the writer I always was into a published writer. Also Cady Vishniac at Reservoir Lit; A. C. Buchanan at Capricious; Caitlin Roper and John Gravois at WIRED; Stephanie Feldman and Nathaniel Popkin, the editors of Who Will Speak For America?; and Brittany Duggan and Andy Sheppard at the IRL Podcast with Mozilla.

Thanks to Marguerite Kenner and Mur Lafferty, whose Space Marine Midwives anthology (sadly not yet come to fruition) pushed me to write "Perpetuation of the Species." Similarly, it was an invitation to write for a horror anthology, a genre I had never written before, that resulted in "The Divided."

Many thanks to everyone who read the stories in process, especially Christopher Thorpe, who provided many insights on "Saint Path" in particular.

As always, I could not have done this without my family: Dora Vázquez Older (who read almost all the stories as drafts); Marc Older; Daniel José Older; Lou Valdez; Calyx Older; and Paz Older.

About the Author

Malka Older is a writer, aid worker, and sociologist. Her science-fiction political thriller *Infomocracy* was named one of the best books of 2016 by Kirkus, Book Riot, and the Washington Post, and shortlisted for the 2019 Neukom Institute Literary Arts Award. With the sequels *Null States* (2017) and *State Tectonics* (2018), she completed the Centenal Cycle trilogy, a finalist for the Hugo Best Series Award of 2018. She is also the creator of the serial *Ninth Step Station*, currently running on Serial Box. Named Senior Fellow for Technology and Risk at the Carnegie Council for Ethics in International Affairs for 2015, she has more than a decade of field experience in humanitarian aid and development. Her doctoral work on the sociology of organizations at Sciences Po Paris explores the dynamics of post-disaster improvisation in governments.

Other Mason Jar Press Titles

Manhunt
a novella by Jaime Fountaine

The Couples
a novella by Nicole Callihan

All Friends Are Necessary
a novella by Tomas Moniz

Continental Breakfast
poetry by Danny Caine

How to Sit
memoir by Tyrese Coleman

Broken Metropolis
an anthology of queer speculative fiction
edited by Dave Ring

I am Not Famous Anymore
poems by Erin Dorney

Learn more at masonjarpress.xyz